Joyce

Also written by Elizabeth / Elle Mitchell

OREGON / INTERCONNECTED WORLD

sweethearts

Janes / standalone series
#1. *Our Tragedy*
#2. *Am I Olive?*
#3. *Another Elizabeth*
#4. *What's Underneath*
#4.5 *Claw Machine*

Their Haunted Bodies / standalone series
#1. *Joyce*

STANDALONE FICTION

I Never Stopped
Fleshy's
The Christmas Villa
American Are You Scared Yet
After the Main Course
Story Rich Art

SERIES

The Miniature Project
#1. *We Used to Be Different*

COOKBOOK

So Simple Soft Foods

MONTHLY POCKET PUBLICATION

The Little Periodical

———

Also edited by ELIZABETH / ELLE MITCHELL

ANTHOLOGIES

Claw Machine
Story Rich Art
Experimental Files

JOYCE

Published in the United States by Little Key Press.

Joyce is a work of fiction. Names, characters, businesses, places, and events are either the product of the author's imagination or are used fictitiously. Any resemblance to actual persons, living or dead, businesses, companies, or events is entirely coincidental.

First Edition

Cover design, embroidery, and photograph by Elizabeth Mitchell
Cover and spine fonts: Adobe Garamond Pro, Gotham Light, Quicksand, Times, and ylee MHIM

Chapter heading images:
papapishu, Firkin, j4p4n, valessiobrito, A. Yoga Perdana, Pheladiii, VintageSnipsandClips, StarGlade, bf5man, raw pixel, GDJ, SeriousTux, kamakalama, ArtsyBee, johnny_automatic, openclipart, Saydung, and Magnilion

For me

Joyce

Content Warning.

This book contains scenes that may challenge you. There is no horror meant in them, just a representation of disability through both a realistic and magical lens.

worn.

Teen Bop posters and glow-in-the-dark stickers haunt the room like ghosts of my past. I told my mother she could change it so many years ago, but the glossy paper still clings by the grace of a few putty wads. Photos of friends I can't remember and a lipstick print on the mirror serve as a reminder that I was once a healthy, vibrant young woman, that I've had breathless dawns on the beach and laughter-filled nights, waiting in line to dance.

This was a place of comfort once. It's not the same. Now that I've aged and the roof is missing shingles, now that the cedar pier has new divots from storms I wasn't here for and fresh growth has made the forest more wild, now that the nearest town noise has risen and occasionally shatters the expected stillness, now that the house is empty, now that she's dead.

The twin bed is uncomfortable. Not just because it's low to the ground or firm from the cold. Memories and nightmares are woven into the fabric—monsters clawing at my feet, a kiss with Henry, my hands over my ears, doing homework, filling out magazine quizzes, screaming myself awake, the first time I listened to a record.

My rarely-used keyboard is shoved in the corner, the bench

seat still hard. Sitting on it now makes my spine hurt, reminding me why I stopped attending practice in the first place. I've forgotten what a G minor is and how much that matters to the act of playing a tune.

I hunt-and-peck at the keys, looking for the right notes. After a few moments, my hands find the proper position, and my knees curl into my chest, like they always did.

It's lucky you don't want to use a Baby Grand, my mother would often say, pointing out my imperfect posture and inability to work pedals with no feet on the ground. I had no desire to learn the piano at all. Never did. She pretended not to understand that.

But now, I'm playing our melody. Or trying. It's not good. Sour notes bash into my brain. Nerve endings at the tips of my fingers burn.

When I taste snot, I stand. There's no proper end, no bowing, no clapping from a humoring teacher, just the melody becoming an echo of itself in my ears.

As it fades, the house picks up where it left off. Never fully silent, it moans and creaks from the witch who's supposedly been burrowed in the walls since long before my mother summered here in the 70s. She's said to always sound old, moody, needy. Though my mother, Dad, Gramms, and Gramps all claim to believe in her, no one ever heard the same thing at the same time. She is either real and speaks to us only when we need her or she is just a story.

I am a lot like the house witch now. Old body, mood swings, needing things I'll never be able to get again. It could be why I have finally found my way into my childhood bedroom. A few days here, and I've slept in the guest bedroom—if only to *avoid*.

Making my way to the bathroom is as routine as brushing my teeth. It's automatic. I ignore the light. I know where things are, and to look at myself is to come face-to-face with loss. I can't see that now, not after being in the room with pink walls and a purple shag rug, the promise of a bright future and lost dreams in every corner.

 ELIZABETH MITCHELL

Toilet paper is in the same poorly laid out place it was when I was a child—barely in reach while sitting down. It's become even more inconvenient now that there seem to be no tissue boxes and my eyes won't stop leaking. I'd carry a roll with me, but my hands always seem to be in use: carrying a blanket, holding the staircase banner and tracing the wall, clutching my ribcage.

The faucet runs freezing, with aging pipes no longer fighting the encroaching Autumn. I wait for the water to warm before splashing my face.

There's still so much to do. Decisions need to be made—ones I should have made already. But I had life to get sorted, things to box and unbox, people to shelve. I knew I needed time before I was of sound mind.

It's barely cracked noon, yet I'm worn down to the nub. My body tells me it's six o'clock, maybe seven. A few hours of life is all I've had lately. The relapse has been hard on me. The grief has been hard on me. The forgetting to eat, forgetting to sleep, forgetting to breathe has been hard on me.

As often happens around this time, my body is trying to shut off.

The question of where to rest for a while nags. The porch swing or the downstairs couch that already has a convenient me-sized shape dug into it, maybe. But the bright popcorn yellow sun streaks across the oak floors, highlights sparkles in the air, and urges me to enjoy it while it lasts. It must not be six after all. My sense of time hasn't been right for quite a while now.

With the last bit of energy I have for the day, I need fresh air. I've always enjoyed bookending my days outside—even in the bustle of the city.

I walk across the deck, past the table for four and Americana grill station. Down three steps, I hit grass. A dozen paces later, I make it to the edge of what constitutes the actual backyard.

Venturing further out is enticing. Just looking at the tree line gives me pause, though. Today is not the day for the woods, the boat shed, the clearing, the pier, *the lake*.

The wind has picked up, my skin has begun to ache as the air rushes over exposed skin, it's colder than I expected. So many reasons to go back in.

Everyone who's met me knows I'm a good liar.

Apparently, that includes to myself.

chilled.

Nightmares plagued me, as they have every night since the lawyer called. Beaks and branches, eyes and screams, bleeding clouds and melting piano keys woke me before the sun. In my old apartment, they saw me sticking my head out of a window to suck lost breath in again; here, I've been able to step outside and inhale forest air to shake the remnants of my fear.

This morning is the same. I must escape the confines of walls and echoes.

Chilled plastic is an iron to my skin. Heat sears along my fingers in the shape of a handle. Dad added the double sliding glass doors for Gramms when this was still her house.

How frustrating these doors were to me during our summers here. A wooden dowel my mother settled in the hollow track to keep me from opening them had me running around the house to go to the lake when I was younger. Seems we will never get along.

I blow on my palms to cool the burn. The pain will ease soon enough.

From the basket of cold weather wear on the floor, I find fleece-lined gloves, then zip into my buttery-soft chocolate leather jacket. I grab the cane I keep beside the door, reach for the handle once again, and tug.

Outside, the sky is neon and cloudless. Red and orange and yellow are sprinkled throughout the branches of the forest below.

Far away birds are cracked pepper on the clouds. To birders like my father, they are *Northern Flickers* or *Black-necked Grebes* or *Pine Siskins*. To me, they are just beautiful nameless creatures to enjoy from the ground.

A few moments outside, and I grow used to the windless crisp air.

Humming a possibly made-up tune, I lose myself in the walk. Without noticing, I've entered the woods and gone so far as to reach the boat shed.

Many afternoons, I would rush to this shed to collect a life preserver to use as a floaty. The key to the padlock was in the kitchen drawer beside the stove, usually lost under menus to places we rarely visited, in a sea of paperclips and rubber bands we never used.

As I near the boat shed, it's hard to miss how it's aged. Nothing goes untouched by time.

Cobwebs decorate corners. Dew drops cling to their intricate lace designs. Green shingles are cracked, crusted with brown and black. A few are missing, similar to the lake house itself. Mold has found its way into the nooks and crannies of the tan siding—another thing I will need to make a decision about.

The lock is missing.

Years of my parents hollering after me to *lock the shed, check on the lock, lock up behind me, remember the key, put the key back* flash in my mind.

My mother could have just tired of searching for the key. It doesn't have to mean anything ominous. The boat shed is in almost the center of the woods, far enough in it would take knowing about it or really looking for something interesting to come across it. And what did it have in it of interest? Nothing.

But the missing lock definitely doesn't have to mean anything. My heart has sped up nonetheless.

Still, despite the cheerful day surrounding me, I pause, listen, wait for something—someone's footfalls, maybe. *Whose*, I'm unsure.

The sounds I hear aren't human. There are cracking branches and hissing bugs.

I take a deep inhale of the sickly sweet scent of mildew, exhale thoughts of eyes on me. My next inhale comes with crushing loss. Compound grief always hovers at the edge of my horizon. The exhale brings another thought—no padlock could mean an empty boat shed. I try to steady myself, just in case.

Hinges creak as I pull the doors wide open. The sun finds her way into the dark space, if only just enough to illuminate shapes and create long shadows. She refuses to be anything less than present today. I appreciate her being with me, keeping time for me, warming my numbed cheeks as I look in the shed.

Not empty. My mother has added things. A thin wooden work bench is on the left wall now. Tools are laid out on the surface impractically. None seem special. One of the wrenches looks handy for around-the-house projects, so I shove it in my jacket pocket. A few things around the cabin need fixing. I don't have plans to fix them, but I've noticed them all the same.

Tucked underneath is the wooden stool I used to annoy my parents with, spinning around and around, making it taller, then shorter. It was once in the corner of the kitchen beside Dad's chair.

The rest of the space is the same. Four life preservers on a metal pole stick out from the back wall. On the right, a wooden structure with giant dowels holds an orange canoe. Beat up oars hang beside it. Usually, at least. Now, there is only one oar—the one I used as a piñata stick. I missed the paper maché candy-filled sunflower, hitting a tree instead. The dent's shadow looks like a stain.

I lean my cane against the inside of the shed. Though I'm not physically up for the task, I try to slide the canoe forward along the dowels.

I don't know how long it will be before this kind of action comes easily again—if it ever will.

Legs wobble, arms burn, but I manage to get it to the edge. Before I can feel triumphant, it tips and falls. I barely step back in time to avoid a crushed foot. As it hits the cement floor, I wait for the crack. A quiet thud greets me. *Good.*

This kind of canoe is supposed to be able to withstand a lot of abuse, after all. Or so I think they said. No one taught me anything about canoeing except how to get in without tipping over and how to get mud off of the seats.

I grab the old towel stuffed inside, lay it on the floor, and begin to wrestle the canoe onto it. With each pull and wriggle, my body protests, reminds me that my relapse isn't over, that if I push, I'll just crash again.

Moving back into the shed to grab the single oar, I notice my shadow growing long and reaching towards the back wall. A shape on either side is familiar—a tall man with a hand reaching mine, a short woman with her head tilted towards me, but never fully reaching.

Little puffs of my breath are visible, a train chugging along. I turn to my right, then to my left. *Alone.* I've been alone all along.

Stepping back into the full sun, I take slower, steady breaths. My mother's words come to mind. *This place is special.*

Special is often a loaded word. This case is no different.

We moved here when I was young enough to find reasons to love it, make friends at the school with a minuscule population, but old enough I understood the reason we were here at all: my mother needed to be surrounded by memories to stop sobbing.

Dad got a job nearby, and we turned Gramms' house—usually associated with cookies and swimming and laughter—into *our* home. My new reality began to involve chores, a lot less time on the water, and tears that never dried.

The hefty, dusty canoe is smushing the forest floor on an old gray-green towel.

Pausing before one acts is important. I've learned that lesson

     ELIZABETH MITCHELL

many times over—often at my detriment. This time, it might stick.

I'll need to see if the canoe still floats. But for now, I need to rest, get some heat on my knees, my tailbone, my back. Perhaps I'll just heat a blanket in the dryer and take a nap swaddled in warmth. Like a womb. Anyone's but my mother's. Hers was hostile to me, a precursor to years of our relationship.

unease.

A falling branch and shattering glass fills the forest. Unease settles beside my grief. No gusts of wind. No recent storms.

A bird may have pecked at the fragile glass of the kitchen window one too many times, desperate to get the bunch of fake grapes collecting dust on the counter. Grumpy, the house witch could have finally decided to demand more of a voice than the creaks and groans everyone has grown accustomed to. It may have even been the sounds of a car crash bouncing from tree to tree, reaching me as the wheels stopped spinning. No reason to imagine anything else.

Still, I lock the sliding doors behind me.

I should call someone, text someone, tell *someone* about this *something*. I'm not sure who, though. Maybe the lawyer who informed me of my mother's will and asked me if I wanted to live here or sell it.

Though I didn't hesitate before, "I'll be there by the end of the week," was flying from my mouth, telling people what I was doing and where I was going, discussing my mother and pain, had barely crossed my mind. I emailed my boss and said I'd be using all of my sick leave and paid time off. I won't be back, but I didn't want the days to go to waste. My ex only knows in case he needs to send me stray mail—folded insults that still say *Mrs.* and know nothing of my losses. I didn't think to call or text a friend, though. Perhaps that speaks to who I find precious in life.

What would I tell this someone anyhow? There was a sound, and I'm jumpy? My body hurts, my mind is in a fog, and now things are Big and Scary?

Besides, my phone has been dead since I got here. The charger is with my laptop and mouse and earbuds and extra bra and specialty Frankenstein coins a friend bought me because I made an off-handed comment about Mary Shelley's talent. Some-place, in a container on a truck or a loading dock, my belongings are making their way to me. I think about them often—especially after hearing there was a delay; something about shipping or tariffs. It's all so hazy now. Grief saw me throwing things I've loved dearly since childhood in the trash, tossing useful items in a box marked FREE, packing trinkets I forgot I had, and keeping things I'm not sure are mine.

I have a feeling I may not unpack what arrives. I'm almost certain I can manage without my collector's edition BunBunn lamp. I don't need that little yellow saucepan intended for milk—and only milk—or my set of scuffed, cheap kitchen knives. Nor do I have use for three decorative salt and pepper shakers or fifteen mugs or any of the other pieces I curated for a life I've left behind. At least, I haven't.

Since I've arrived, I've only needed blankets and pillows, one large pan and a mug, my toothbrush and toothpaste, soap, a wash-cloth, and a towel—all of which she had.

My mother left me the house and everything in it.

She left me grief and memories, too.

I've needed rest and space to cry. My apartment didn't have that. There was a pillow with ripped stitches and vague imprints left by my teeth as I tried to bite my anger away. There was a kitchen floor covered in broken dishes and a bed too hard to swaddle me. Every room I escaped to came with noises from a neighbor.

I just needed the calm and quiet. Not the stuff or the people.

All I want to do is to tip over. Instead, I go about the arduous process of checking every door and window to see which was broken, keeping my fingers crossed that I can manage not fixing it for a while.

Downstairs, there is a half-bath with no window next to a very small room my mother used for sewing but is now filled with junk and tarps and dust. It has a large window that looks out towards the driveway and the woods in front of the house.

Checking that room yields nothing but lungs in distress and me hacking up floating motes.

While in the kitchen, I turn off the oven. *Wonder how long it's been on.* I'm not sure when I last ate.

Undamaged, the two windows are open wide for fresh air. I pull them closed with a mix of disappointment and relief.

The dining room sliding doors are still locked. By now, they may be sealed shut from not being opened in ages. I grab a dirty plate from the table, put the cap back on the gray nail polish I was using last night, turn off the table lamp I brought in from the living room.

Upstairs, I check the guest room I'm staying in. It's the first room on the left. More dust clings to the edges of the chipped window frame. The screen is ripped right in the center, but the glass is unbroken.

My childhood bedroom has streaky double windows. The screens are missing, having been popped out long ago when I tried to sneak out—only to find there was no eave below me, no tree for me to climb out, no high school TV moment I could create.

The bathroom's half rippled glass window is also fine. A small fracture at the bottom left that's been here since I was a child hasn't changed. Like a wrinkle on a ninety-year-old, it's stayed the same size.

Only my mother's room remains. *My mother's remains.*

My arm moves to knock, but I remember in time. The handle is tough to turn, weak as I am.

Adding insult, the door feels sticky as I push it. Usually, this is rainy weather behavior for the swelling wood. Now, it's just me.

My parents' bed sits right under the window.

The mattress that saw fifteen years of goodnight kisses and me sneaking in to stave off the monsters and held space for love and anger and friendship should be covered in fractured glass. The window is intact, as is the mirror in their en suite. These were the last possible pieces large enough to make the shattering noise.

But nothing is broken.

The sound was just a sound.

I check that this window is locked nonetheless, then slink down the hall to the guest room again.

When I eventually make my way to the hardware store, I can remodel the master bedroom and move in there—*after* the confusion and grief that's still hanging heavy in the air eases.

Maybe. Perhaps. Possibly.

Not now.

lost.

A dying sun and cool evening breeze sneaks in through a wonky doorframe.

The wind moves me to reach for a second throw. Wrapping it around myself is a warm hug I haven't had in a long time.

My ex-husband almost managed to give me enough love. But ultimately, the lines between love, lust, friendship, companionship, convenience, and hatred were thinner than layers of a spekkoek, and it was nearly impossible to discern what was real or what balance of which we had. I needed to be able to say *I love you* and be sure I meant it.

Lust and I have danced since. But I've found no love.

My stomach grumbles.

I've lost time.

There's some carrot soup still in the fridge from last week. Hot and smooth sounds good right about now.

Socked feet slip a little on a wooden floor that creaks no matter if I move lightly or stick to one side or skip the third step.

A heavy cream-colored blanket drags behind me, creating a woven cape. I imagine a crowd in front of me, cheering my arrival.

Never have I had such fanfare.

Dad thought I should be an actress, with my ability to fake cry and scream rivaling the 80s Scream Queens. But with my mother's prolonged grief suffocating me, I was lucky to make it to college with a vocal cord intact. Using it for entertainment was out of the question.

The electric burner *clicks* as I turn it on. The *tick, tick, tick* reverberates through the u-shaped rectangle filled with stacks of dirty dishes, unpacked grocery bags, an open carton of half and half, and a sliced grapefruit on a cutting board with a fly sitting on the edge. Butane ignites, and a blue flame appears.

I pull the uncovered saucepan from the refrigerator. A burnt orange skin has formed over the soup. With a stained wooden spoon that was once a grand-someone's, I push the film down into the center and stir.

Lost in the rhythmic motion, time slips away once again.

The soup is smoking. Outside is dark, and though the kitchen window is wide open, I can't picture myself unlatching it or tugging it open.

One moment, it's daylight. The next, night is creeping in. One moment, I'm sitting on the couch reading a book. The next, I'm washing my hair.

My blanket is nowhere to be seen. I shiver as I take the pan from the heat and grab a hot pad. I'll skip the bowl tonight. Fatigue and pain settling in throughout my muscles tell me I shouldn't be up and around too much longer. I've clearly been standing here for a while.

The living room couch finds me, and I collapse onto it. There's a tepid water waiting on the too-short coffee table. I appreciate the forethought I had.

shaky.

Throbbing in my hand jerks me away from wherever I went, grounds me in the here.

Divots in my palm from clenched fists remind me of a night I'll never forget. Demanding my attention, I'm drawn backwards to a memory that never seems far away, despite my ignoring it.

He is calm, his tone clipped. I'm embarrassed, apologizing to the woman at the pickup window. It's the last straw, my breaking point. Leaving is my only option. A small leather purse and a cane in one hand, keys to my car and a plastic bag with the three paper bags of medicine we just picked up in the other, I walk away from him.

I'm not holding anything now. Recently painted nails are curled into tender flesh. In this moment, my allodynia is intense —every nerve ending is hyper-sensitive and a razor's edge away from pain no matter what I do. If a breeze wafts in through a broken window seal or I stand too close to a small heater, I may be taken down.

The remainder of the carrot soup is on the blanket in a globby puddle. No burns from the saucepan, at least—on me or the comforter. It's the *Little things*.

Dragging the weight of three toddlers, I make my way towards the laundry room. As I toss the blanket into the pile of dirty laundry that's not too old, something shiny on the floor catches my attention lying next to a pair of navy sweatpants.

Takes me a few seconds to bend, but eventually I manage to touch chilled metal. *My engagement ring.* Last I saw this, I was stuffing it between two blankets I wanted here before the rest of my things. I haven't been able to shuck the band off, but that's more out of comfort than anything.

I've yet to need those blankets, so the suitcase has remained unzipped in the closet upstairs. That should mean the ring hasn't moved either.

A lump rises to my throat. *The shattered glass.*

Bizarre. Nonsense.

And yet, it's with shaky hands that I start the washing machine, trying to think of anything but the unsettling nature of being alone here. Or just being alone for the first time in so long.

My wedding doesn't give me strong feelings, nor does most of our marriage—just flashes of laughs and kisses, bruised knuckles and crying in the bathroom, grieving beside each other with no language to comfort one another, and a necessary, but devastating end. Sad to lose a friend of any kind for reasons beyond one's control. Especially so when I've been deemed *lacking.*

The stone on the engagement ring makes me think of my mother's diamonds, her curated collection of jewelry, her jewelry box.

It was sent to me in my old apartment. My mother told the lawyers that my decision to move here or not didn't matter. I had to have the jewelry box the day after she died.

I couldn't open it, wasn't ready.

There were more pressing things to do when I arrived here. Like manage the still raw pain from my Dad's absence, accept the ripples of grief my mother left behind as I grappled with my own, and settle in to my new—but not new—home and reality.

Still, I haven't opened it. The jewelry box is so much more than wood covered in pink satin.

I recall every piece and which slot it's in.

Top left is a round lapis brooch. Never fitting properly, it stands upright at an angle. My mother wore it once in my memory—to a potluck at school. Other moms wore pencils and apples, but she strode in with a look of sophistication out of place for the event. When I made an off-handed comment about it, she flung it across the room. Whether it was my tone or the verbiage, I don't know, but she never did believe I was complimenting her.

Settled beside it is an oval gray topaz ring that was too large for my mother's thin fingers—fingers meant to play piano in a way I could barely dream of, if I had ever dreamed of concert halls and black dresses and canceling plans to practice for recitals. The gold band is so delicate, she was always afraid to resize it. It would fit me, I imagine. One of two heirlooms, I wonder if wearing it would make me feel more connected to my family or cursed by the loss.

A gold seashell charm with a pink pearl sits in the top center slot, its dainty chain in the space beside it. Gramms passed it down to my mother on Christmas. I was seven or eight. They cried together. Naively, I thought we would have that moment one day.

Top right is her only costume piece: a faux emerald four-leaf clover ring Dad gave her the day I was born that all but assured my middle name wouldn't be DeeDee, as my mother had always planned it to be.

The story of his giving her the four-leaf clover became a tall tale, told differently every time—even to the same person. The moment my mother shouted that her water broke, Dad grabbed the ring—before the go-bag. *Or* he left her in the car to rush back in and get it. At the hospital, moments after the first push, he presented her with the ring and a kiss on the head. *Or*, when the doctor announced he could see my head, he opened the ring box and told her he loved her. With her next *big push*, she nearly shattered his hand with the box in it. *Or* she told him to give it to her later when her hands weren't swollen. *Or* all of this took place on the way to the hospital at a stoplight. *Or* before her water broke.

Or hours after I was born—and moments before they had to sign off on my name—Dad admitted that he hated the name DeeDee and gave my mother the ring.

We all had our guesses as to what really happened, but it's just lore now.

The import of the ring didn't earn it a place on her finger, though. I always wondered why.

My mother's diamonds were given the center row—two karat studs, tear drop earrings, tennis bracelet, first engagement ring, and a heart charm.

The third, bottom row has only two long spaces that contain her two more precious pieces. They are the ones she wore every time she left the house and the reason I'm unable to open the box. I'm not ready to see them in person again.

She requested not to be cremated with any of them. So they are there, waiting.

safe.

Birds peck at my eyes. They squawk in my face. *You should remember us.*

Forcing myself awake, I yank the sheets off my legs and hop out of bed. I get ready for the day quicker than is comfortable.

Downstairs, I open the front entrance closet and am taken aback to see three rain coats, three cold weather coats, three pairs of rain boots, three umbrellas, three sets of binoculars, a book on identifying birds, and a box of ephemera from the few trips the family went. My mother was never able to clean it out, let Dad's things go. Or mine, it seems. The sizes are a time capsule of *before grief.* Adult man size large, shoe size 11. Adult woman size medium, shoe size 5 1/2. Child size large, shoe size 4. She replaced my teenaged boots for ones from when I was six, maybe seven.

My umbrella is a dainty, polka-dotted thing with frills around the edges. My mother's is practical and basic black, as small as her shoe size. Dad's is wider, thicker, built for bad weather.

I slide on my mother's coat. Her scent surrounds me. I pause, listen for another smash of glass. Maybe I got it wrong, and it was her all along.

Silence and the warble of something outside answers me.

I find myself nodding and huffing through my nose. Another type of resignation. *Of course it's not her.*

Going further out, I can't wear my barely-more-than-fashion boots. My father's rain boots fit better than my mother's—so petite I couldn't wear her shoes by the time she bought me that frilly umbrella. So I wear his. There is plenty of room in the boots, so much I'll clomp, not walk. I become the girl from this archival closet who played Business Woman, wearing my mother's dress, Dad's shoes, and Gramms' pearls—they had since been passed down to my mother. And now, to me, I suppose.

Weatherproofed, I collect Dad's birding book and binoculars before closing the door softly. The sound mirrors me snuffing out a sob.

Vaguely remembering one of the many sage phrases my parents had about being prepared and comfort in the wilderness, I pack a peanut butter sandwich, fill a water bottle, and grab a blanket from the basket, then tuck it all in Dad's rucksack that still hangs on the back of his chair in the kitchen like so many other fragments of his ghost.

The floorboards settle noisily with my heavy footfalls—or the house witch is at work again.

With roots and fallen branches, living beings and small mammals underfoot, I move strategically rather than quickly.

The woods welcome me, as expected. Foliage crunches beneath my weight. Puddles settled in hidden hollow divots splash up around my boots. Morning air under the canopy is freezing. And for once in a long time, I'm given the gift of nerves not catching on fire with the drop in temperature.

Still, I shiver. *Almost there.*

When I reach the clearing, I'm sweaty and out of breath. My muscles sag.

But, positioned beside Gramms' feathered friend graveyard,

his bench awaits. Handmade, my initials are carved in the right arm, his in the left. The whole thing is imperfect and beautiful.

The back legs are just a bit shorter than the front, and the seat slats are uneven, creating a fairly painful sitting experience. Dad pretended it was on purpose. *So it was obviously handmade. So we could see the birds better. So we wouldn't stay in one place too long.*

He was an explorer trapped in one block. Slow, quiet, careful to respect the animals' space, with a hefty dose of curiosity.

The bench is even more uncomfortable to this body I'm still adjusting to—fatigued and easily pushed past its limits.

Pulling the blanket from the tan canvas bag, I waffle. *Warmth or comfort? Under or over? Over or under?* I fold it three times and slide it under me. It evens out the seat some.

Here, in Dad's favorite place, with his bag open, his binoculars in hand, I can smell him. His aftershave mingles with dying leaves.

Dad's hand grips my shoulder. I lean towards it. My head rests against his arm, so like we used to do.

A rhythmic warbling rattle makes me jump, and my elbow crashes into the crooked slatted backrest. I whip around, gasping.

Warm and strong, his grip releases and leaves an imprint that grows cold.

A blue-bodied, black-headed feathered babe testing my nerves is the first I see in Dad's clearing. No binoculars required for this one. I think it's a jay of some kind.

I rip open the birding book and begin flipping. Page after page cuts into tingling, pink fingers. There was a trick to this, I think —a way to find them before they fly away.

Dad's voice is muffled as he talks about improving his birding skills. The memory is coated in a morning fog. I've replaced it with moments of sitting in front of a dial-up computer with annoyance, jingles from carpet commercials, alternative routes home to avoid traffic, quotes from famous people, my favorite memes, names of colors—all meaningless junk now.

Passing a photo of a small, stocky bird with emerald feathers,

I land on a photo of a similar shape and color to my possible new friend. The glossy page has Dad's smudged fingerprints at the edges, as most do.

For only a moment, I study it. The feathers on the top of the head seem right. It says it's often in Corbam County. So, possibly.

I glance up for comparison. *Are you a—*

The bird has flown away. Unless I see them again, I'll never know if they were a Steller's Jay or not.

Knowing the species of birds we were looking at was Dad's hobby. Simply enjoying them may be mine. Scrambling through a one-inch thick book filled with superfluous information about backyard feeders, neighborhoods, statistics, and maps doesn't hold the promise of joy I saw Dad have. His eyes would light up as he'd touch the image and point. *Discovery is a great interim for adventure,* he'd say.

Maybe I'm meant to find the peace that was stolen from me in this clearing. I will know the birds in my own way as I settle in.

I can never go back to the place I thought of as home. The longer I'm here, the more it's as if that's an old skin I'm sloughing off.

Clusters of birds fly into the trees and settle on thin branches. They exchange pleasantries. That was one of Dad's favorite sounds. He'd tweet back at them and wait, listen.

I raise the binoculars to my eyes and scan the shedding trees.

Gray birds with burnt orange tummies perform an upbeat concert just for me. A few are fluffier than others. Perhaps growing extra feathers for warmth, as I remember Dad telling me I couldn't do—his reasoning for why I needed to wear a sweater, a jacket, *and* a coat on the coldest days.

From morning till dusk, I watch them, and they watch me. Enthralled, I compartmentalize the ache that crawls up my back. Their eyes peeking from between foliage give me that uneasy feeling again. But they're just animals. By the boathouse... that was something *different*.

Two small birds perch on the arm of the bench beside Dad's

    ELIZABETH MITCHELL

carved initials. Little black heads with white cheeks and more black under their beaks.

None have gotten this close, sat for so long. They've been studying me as much as I've been simply enjoying them.

One has a crooked beak. The other tilts their head to the left. I can't tell if it's from curiosity or if, like me, their body is different—mine on the inside, theirs on the out.

Once, I saw a thick-necked squirrel run across the yard. They ran in a zigzag pattern, pausing every so often to reorient to the direction they wanted to go. Was it a birth defect? Or a broken neck from a fall corrected by nature? Modern medicine doesn't exist in the forest, but healing does.

The two birds settle as I think about the kindred squirrel. They get as comfortable as I'm not.

Long shadows play tag with the clutter on the clearing's floor. Another day has come and gone.

Crooked Beak hops from the arm and lands on my knee. Mouth wide, they let out one piercing note of their song, then fly off. Their companion stands. Smoky vellum wings open, and they take flight.

They won't peck at me anymore—the birds. Not in my dreams, not in reality.

It's okay that I don't remember their names or what they eat. I don't need to know the proper classification of each. I only need to know *them*. And in time, I will.

They will accept me now, keep me safe.

Dad's sigh behind me is almost a chuckle. He's right. That is too much to ask of them, of anyone. At least so soon. No one is safe. He taught me that.

I'll be back soon, little ones, I think as I walk away from the many species in the trees.

tense.

In the kitchen making breakfast, I hear a thud at the front door. Definitely not a knock. Knocks are different—thinner, lighter.

As I move to the foyer, I imagine a tree branch stretched from its trunk, a monster with seven eyes, or a wolf with slick hair and a pearly grin. My muscles tense as a long-lost memory of someone pushing their way into my first apartment on a windy Thursday evening threatens to invade my scarred heart. So long ago. But the body remembers.

The house witch moans, and the wooden floor softens and ripples.

Through the peephole, I see the back of a young girl with a bag slung over her shoulder. She's hopping on a mint chocolate chip ice cream bike.

I step out in socked feet, just as she begins to pedal away. Her long red-brown hair flying behind her is so similar to mine, I feel haunted.

A hole in the woven fabric of my sock has my heel touching something other than a bristle mat. Glancing down, I see a newspaper.

Picking it up takes a lot of effort. It feels as if I've been on the floor scrubbing or exercising.

The headline of the Tillus Observer says a fisher saved a little girl. The last headline I read was from the Janes Chronicle. It mentioned six missing girls. What a difference an hour and a half drive can make.

I notice that it's Tuesday the 14th. I would have sworn it was... a Friday? Probably the 3rd or 5th.

Days are slipping by.

But the date is good to know. *Grounding*, as my old therapist would say. This is the first paper that's come.

Have I really only been here a week?

I could have recycled the last one, though I don't remember doing that. In the haze of arrival and existing and sobbing, it still seems plausible.

I won't cancel the newspaper, if not just for something new to read every week.

jostled.

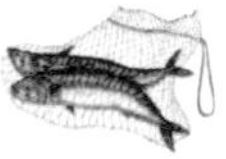

A rundown teal house acts as both the hardware store and small bait shop—not the one you'd use if you were going on a long fishing trip. That one is further into town. This is the one Dad always used. Gramms said she'd been going to it since she was a little girl.

Once simply called *Bait Shop*, its sign now reads *Lois' Bait Shop*.

Four dirt and gravel parking spots pockmarked with divots are on the left side. A cement pad of six spots with roots breaking free from its center is on the right. I end up in the farthest dirt spot.

Naturally, my wheel falls into a deep hole as I pull in.

With a jostled spine and irritation, I steel myself for speaking to someone.

Even just walking to the front door, I feel like an outsider, despite spending most of my life in the house on the lake. It was nearly as rundown as this place when we first moved in—after Gramms died.

In a knit sweater and jeans, my clothes are out of place, out of time. They are not rugged, not practical. The pieces are thinner, soft, not designed to withstand bending and scraping and bumping, dirt or brambles or even tall grass.

"Hey, there! How can I help you today?" a woman asks.

She's wearing an olive green canvas work apron over jeans and a black long-sleeved shirt with a name tag that reads, *Lois*. The owner.

Lois is all round cheeks, as if she's just happy to be here. Few people are really this happy.

As I figure out the best way to formulate words, I take in the store. So unlike its outside, the space is bright with light wood floors. Lacquered fish frozen in mid-swim—with hooks in their mouths and sides, missing fins, and smears of blood—hang beside rusty antique signs that boast about handymen *getting the job done* and tell of the many reasons one should *beware*.

It's all curated—evenly spaced in an ombre of woodsy colors. The approachable lightness is broken up by the decor seemingly meant to set the hunters and fishers at ease. Unless this is just Lois' taste. Her home may be filled with taxidermy and a polished gun case inscribed to her.

I don't want to answer her question. I want to roam, find the padlock on my own, find a *canoe fixing kit* beside it. But small towns don't operate that way. I may not know these people, but I remember the mentality that has me labeled 'stranger', one to watch. Only a conversation will allow that brand to be removed.

"Hi. I need a padlock," I say—*croak*, really. When her eyes don't fill me with the same stomach-clenching feeling I felt in the woods, I continue. "And do you know anything about fixing a canoe?" My throat is raw as I speak. It's been a while since I've said anything out loud. "Fiberglass, I think. There's a crack that I may or may not have caused when I dropped it—or it fell, really. Could have been there for a long time, though. Hasn't been touched in years. I'll also need an oar."

Lois nods, smirks. "Just *one*?" Despite only saying two words, it's clear she speaks in bubble letters.

I want to pop them as she raises a dark, thick, natural eyebrow. I imagine her mother didn't teach her to tweeze when she was nine.

     ELIZABETH MITCHELL

A flash of jealousy pangs as I picture a childhood with a mother who brushed my hair and told me I was beautiful just as I was.

"Well, as long as a dented one works fine. Otherwise..." I trail off.

"You can certainly repair them."

"One project is all I have in me. I'll get a set of oars, I guess. And whatever I need to fix my canoe—including *very* detailed instructions, if you have them. I'm without internet at the moment." Even to another woman, I can't help but to explain myself just a little.

"Absolutely."

She takes me around the store, grabbing items from the many rows and full shelves with labels made of large wood slices. Burned into each, they tell customers the categories: *paint*, *glue*, *wrenches*, *bolts*. The organization has married the old and the new. It doesn't feel like it did when I was small, when a man with a crooked smile and sour breath named Sidney ran it. Back then, it was a curio shop of teetering hooks, plastic fish, and handsaws.

Were you related to Sidney? I ask Lois in the conversation I'm not willing—or able—to have with her.

She tells me, and we talk about how odd and lovely he was. The story of how she ended up with this place is more harrowing than expected; there is love and magic and bloodshed.

"You'll need this." Lois' voice deflates my running imagination. Grabbing one thing and tucking it into her large apron pocket. "Also, this."

I don't see what either *this* or *this* is, but of course I'll need them. Nodding along with her choices, I'm admiring the punched tin lighting and netting ceiling decor. Fish are caught in the net, and like the ones on wall placards, they are in mid-flail.

Lois pauses at an empty row on the shelf and tilts her head. She calls over her shoulder to someone that's yet to be seen, "Kurt, honey? Do we have any release film? Thought I ordered some a few months ago. Don't remember selling any."

A disembodied voice responds, "I'll look!"

Lois writes down steps for me while Kurt heads back to investigate.

He hasn't made an appearance by the time she finishes, and I'm panicking a little. I see idle chitchat in the future and picture myself turning into an actual flounder, flopping so hard on the wooden floor that my scales begin to scrape off. I'd leave a shiny, bloodied trail of *me* as I race towards the exit.

Would Lois mount my mangled body? Soft mouth open in a *glorp* face, the whole of me would fit in the empty, waiting space by the exit sign.

"So, you—"

"Got it!" Kurt shouts, jogging towards us. Blue eyes glitter as a short young man waves a package clutched in his hand. "Just hadn't gotten to the box yet."

My scales can remain intact.

"Well, looks like that's everything then! Let's get you checked out."

On my way to the exit, Lois exploits my slow walking speed to rush from behind the counter. Her hug almost knocks me over, but she seems careful not to squeeze or cause me to drop my bag or oars. Her kindness and consideration catch me off-guard.

Misjudging people is a specialty of mine. Often, I'm too open, too trusting, too accepting. But she could be who she appears to be.

"Your mother was a beautiful soul. And I have a feeling you take after her. I look forward to hearing how this goes!"

She's known who I was this whole time?

"Kurt!" Lois shouts. "Take these oars to Joyce's car."

Stunned, my chest constricts.

Because she knows my name? Because she thinks I take after the best parts of my mother? Because a man is taking something from my awkward grasp without asking? Because I'm left wondering what Lois' eyes look like hidden in the trees?

     ELIZABETH MITCHELL

Choked up, I'm only able to raise my plastic bag and smile as I leave, Kurt following behind me in silence.

fatigue.

I can't wait to get the new oars out on the water. There must have been a time when Gramms and Gramps thought the same thing, back when they had a different canoe and were spry. *How many sets of oars ago was that?*

If the canoe wasn't cracked, I would make my way to the lake for a lap or two; if I didn't need to drag it to the lake myself, I would have already done that probably—are just two of the lies I tell myself.

Dropping the bag of supplies and oars on the front porch, I wrap around the house to the backyard.

Something small and gray and unmoving catches my attention. Beside withered flowers I know nothing about, a mouse took its last breath. The tears suddenly warming my eyes surprise me.

I'll come back for you, little one. You deserve a place to rest. The grave-yard will extend beyond feathers now that I'm here.

Onward, I walk through the backyard patio and into the woods, past the boathouse, further than I've been able to go before.

The edge of the pier comes into view, and my feet slow with no conscious thought. Dad's face is there. I hear splashes. A scream.

Listening to my thudding heart, fatigue washes over me. From the trip. From talking to Lois. From making it this far. From seeing the pier.

No longer are my feet the problem. Jelly legs cause me to stumble into a large tree. Soggy bark with still-hard edges bites into my palm. A vivid clover pops from within the broken bits, and I find myself smiling a little, despite the pain.

Then, I notice my hands. *No*, not mine. But familiar.

Bones stretched over thin skin are creased and cracked. Bright bolts of blue and purple veins protrude. Age spots nestle at my wrist, and there's a soft brown mole by my left thumb joint. One short gray hair sticks out from its center.

Gramms held my hand with *these very hands* when she told me stories. Whether a young girl was prancing in the woods or the house witch was protecting us, whether the stars were ancestors or dogs were teaching a school of children manners, at least one of her hands was wrapped around mine. Her sparkling green eyes were locked on the listener's as she spoke.

A storyteller more than anything, she rarely used the books I asked her to read me. She'd have them memorized in her own way by bedtime. The book would be settled in her lap, open to the first page the entire time, so she *didn't have to let me go*.

Touch was such an important part of the narrative to her.

My mother grew up with this. The specialness was lost on her.

Once, on our pier, she told me how she tired of Gramms' stories.

"She'd tell them to my friends when they came over." Leaning back, the sun illuminated my mother's face, and a glimpse of her as a younger woman came into focus. Before marriage or me or grief.

I planned to say, *that sounds like Gramms*. But my mother was lost in a space I couldn't reach.

"If she wasn't holding my hand, she'd hold one of theirs." My mother paused, sighed. "It was frustrating, embarrassing. She never thought of me, though, did she? And *oh*, how Gramms

     ELIZABETH MITCHELL

loved your dad from the jump. When I told her how we met, she added that to the collection of stories she'd tell. As if it was hers. After she actually met him, she seemed to think all of our stories were hers. I'd hear her telling bits and pieces of our lives to her friends, *my* friends, strangers—always holding their hand."

My mother's serene face hardened for a moment.

Then, she swept into a retelling of how she and Dad met. So like her own mother sometimes, my mother. If only she had seen it.

The creases by her thin mouth and moody sky eyes softened. Being just Anne for a moment again, sharing bits of her truest self with me, brightened my mother.

parents.

Anne was as sour as the gray clouds covering the last dredges of the sunset. She should've been happy, with a nice slice of chocolate cake and espresso in front of her. She should've been on the covered patio shouting over the rain. She should've been laughing, brushing her date's arm, fluttering her eyelashes. She should've been talking about staying longer because the weather was so bad.

Instead, she was hiding in the restaurant bathroom. She'd snuck in to throw away the remnants of steak her date had ordered for her—medium, not rare like she likes. To add insult, he'd made her pay for it and insisted on getting the gristle packed up *in a doggie bag*.

Outside the restroom door, he waited for her.

When she'd gone in, he started whistling. Anne couldn't stand whistling. The sound bypassed her ears and grated her nerves like moldy Parm.

"Where's your food?" he asked before she'd fully stepped out.

"It fell."

"Was the box still closed?"

If Anne had any doubt before, she knew then that she had *not* found her future husband.

"Nice meeting you," she said, shoving her hand in front of her.

"You too." The sadness in his eyes seemed disproportionate to the time they'd spent together, the fun they'd had, how much they'd gotten to know each other. "I had a—"

"Actually, I have to go back in." She motioned towards the bathroom. "You can head out. I'll get a cab."

He knew she painted for fun and very little else. Anne wasn't sure why he hadn't left already.

She waited for five minutes before peeking out. He'd gone, to her relief.

Anne missed the small window between heavy clouds holding back and the bottom falling out. It was pouring, and she had no umbrella.

Mere steps outside the restaurant, a bright yellow beacon of hope awaited her.

She rushed to the taxi, rain flattening curls that had been in hot rollers for the better part of the afternoon.

A man careened into her side, tan suede trench coat tugged up and over his head. His fogged glasses hid his expression.

"I need to get home," she said, as if his needs were unimportant.

And to her, they were. She just needed to be anywhere else—to cry, maybe. Another failed date. She was not getting any younger.

"I just had an awful date. Can we share?" the stranger with a baritone voice asked.

Begrudgingly, Anne agreed. Her blue—no, *purple*—satin dress and leather pumps were hand-me-downs, but she still didn't want to see them ruined.

"Okay."

The door opened wider. "After you."

Anne scooted in the cab, telling the cabbie where she lived as she did.

"She was awful," the man said, closing the door behind him. "79th and Grish, for me, please."

 ELIZABETH MITCHELL

Brushing water from her chilled arms, Anne didn't turn his way. "Who was awful?" She asked out of instinct more than interest.

"My date. I couldn't even keep it up til dessert. She had no interest in getting to know me or letting me get to know her. She answered every question I asked with no more than a few words. I was glad to start eating. At least then, the silence made sense. But I chose the place for the chocolate cake, and I didn't get any. I'm more disappointed about that than it not working out with the woman."

Is he a mind reader? Anne wondered, but only said, "My date was also dreadful and left me wanting cake."

"There's a cute Italian bakery a few blocks from here."

The cab slowed a little, the driver giving Anne time to change her destination, maybe. Avoiding a cat in the road was the more obvious and realistic option. But a cabbie with a romantic streak sounded better.

"Okay," Anne said.

"I'm Henry."

Anne finally turned to look at the mystery man fully. More than glasses and a trench coat now, he was a soft jaw and a sharp nose, full lips, thick eyebrows, and two freckles by his left ear.

Yellow street lights flashed across his face before their absence hid him in darkness, making everything else about him stay a mystery. Was the hint of a beard just shadow?

Anne wanted to know the color of his eyes more than anything, see if they pierced in the daytime as much as they did as he met her gaze in the cab that seemed smaller than it was before.

Three blocks later, there was a neon *Open* sign. Henry noticed the Hours of Operation on the glass door said they closed at 8. They were cutting it close, surely.

Open went dark.

Anne and Henry rushed to the door, knocking before the woman turned the lock. All but two lights were already turned off inside.

"Could we sneak in?" Henry asked. "We have cash."

The young woman swiveled from Henry to Anne. She wore a party dress that sparkled in the low light, but she still smiled as she said, "If you order quickly."

Nothing in the bakery had been put away for the night. Anne imagined owning her own bakery for a moment. With her life, the baked goods would rarely get put away until well after 1am. She'd work, go out to enjoy her evening, then she'd come back to close up properly.

If she and Henry were lucky and had just met someone like her, they'd end up with cake.

Anne spoke first. "Do you have two slices of chocolate cake? Any kind of chocolate cake."

The longer they took, the later the woman would be to whatever event she was on her way to attend. Anne didn't want to be picky.

"We do. Torta Caprese."

"Two of those would be perfect."

"Great," she said, putting two pieces of chocolate goodness covered in powdered sugar and two forks into one box—a box that wouldn't end up in a bathroom trashcan.

Henry set a bill on the counter, told the woman to keep the change, and collected the box.

"Thanks for stopping by tonight!" The woman closed the case with a smile. "Have a great evening, you two. You make a lovely couple."

Henry stood a little taller as he held the door open for a blushing Anne.

She wanted to tell the woman they weren't a couple *yet*.

But he answered for them both. "We do, don't we?" he called over his shoulder. Turning to Anne, he asked, "Where to? Looks like you can't get rid of me just yet."

She didn't want to.

"There's a bench right there," Anne suggested.

       ELIZABETH MITCHELL

"It's in the rain," Henry said.

"Worried the chocolate cake will melt?"

Henry laughed, and his gaze met hers. "No. Right now, I'm not worried about anything."

forever.

I remember Dad coming up behind us as my mother finished her story. His long shadow filled the space between us.

"Since our accidental date night, we haven't spent more than a week apart," he added, dropping a kiss on my mother's head.

Her hand reached up and held the side of his face for a moment before they parted. She looked radiant in that moment—loved, loving, kind. I wanted to know that version of her.

I still think about how beautiful their love story was. Gramms and Gramps' beginning wasn't so movie-like, but their love lasted until death did part them. As did my Nans and Paps. I don't know about my great-great grandmother, but something tells me...

It's why I clung to my ex-husband so hard. It's why I told myself it was okay that he had a temper, that it wasn't perfect.

Forever has run in my family for generations. I figured there was something wrong with me if I couldn't make it work.

It never occurred to me that forever love doesn't have to come early, that forever love doesn't have to come with a husband. It never occurred to me that I could be enough for myself, that maybe our family line could stop with me by choice. I've told other friends that—*you don't have to get married, have babies, put up with that shit, do things you don't want to.* But there are different rules for me, right?

Here, weak against a tree, staring at a lake filled with much more than water, I know without a doubt that life is too precious to accept anything but radiance.

I look at my hands—my *Gramms'* hands—trying to recall the details of a story she once told me about time standing still.

But she is no longer in the woods with me.

Thin skin with prominent blue veins—a sculptor's dream—and freckles along three fingers have returned. The hands are mine and mine alone again.

With only my skeleton propelling me forward, I move on legs filled with pudding towards a home of more memories, more ghosts, and a witch that has much to tell me.

     ELIZABETH MITCHELL

open.

In my softest knit, I collect a chunky blanket for my shoulders and slip Dad's boots on.

The birds sing together as I make my way to the forest, humming along.

Just inside the tree line, I find myself tumbling towards the leaves. *Not again.*

But *no.* I've just tripped.

I release my cane without thinking, still not used to it being an aid in all things, and catch myself with brute force to my palms moments before bone crashes into the ground. My knees only graze a root.

I can't hold myself up for long. Though, truly, I don't want to.

Here on the ground, with a spreading ache and a dampness soaking through my leggings, I become a living part of the woods.

Sun beams flash to the thrumming in my body between trees, swaying and shedding themselves of the dead.

In a small, unseen windstorm, those leaves swirl my way and collapse in front of me in a row of long pale yellows and oranges and short dark reds and browns in an all too familiar pattern—piano keys.

I want to play. Straightening and leaning forward slowly, trying to focus on what's in front of me and not the pain, my fingers find their places on the branch adornments.

As I press them, I feel the heft of real keys and hear the true resonate tones one expects from an upright piano far nicer than my keyboard.

Playing our melody again, I expect the same sour timbre as before. It's a simple thing from a music box Gramms gave my mother, a tune that reminded me of the rare moments she tucked me in, told me she loved me, kissed away my tears, sat on the edge of my bed after Dad died and held my hand.

My mind goes away, and my fingers find the memory. Notes slip from under the leaves and rise towards the canopy, imprinting shapes on the wind, as if the air itself is sheet music.

I hear one *caw* and look up. Settled in the surrounding branches, birds act as audience to my performance. Their heads follow the eighth note floating high above us, with half notes trailing behind.

In small moments of pause, they turn their attention back to me.

Closing my eyes, I get lost once again, and play the melody twice, swaying, crying, *breathing*.

When I finally crack my eyes open, I watch the balloon of musical notes pop as I finish the tune and lean back.

The birds screech and tweet and cheer and sing and ask for an ovation I can't give.

My head is splitting open. A migraine approaches me like a hungry, scared animal—tentative but needy enough to risk every-thing. Bent at one angle for too long, I should have expected this. Suddenly, the rest of my body is numb. All signs of my fall have melted away.

I drop my neck backwards as my eyes water—my only outward sign of distress.

A sense of release comes with a *bink, bink, bink, bink, bink*. It's like fat raindrops on a roof. Something has bounced off the log behind me.

   ELIZABETH MITCHELL

I turn to see shiny white things sprawled along the leaves and ground. These came from inside me, the birds tell me.

Walking my fingers through my greasy hair, I find smooth bone. Groping down, I expect to touch a muscly sponge, slick and slimy. Nothingness greets me.

I'm hollow, save a few round things. I tilt back further. The little objects roll towards the edge of my skull to join their friends. The sound matches the *bink* from before.

Bringing one of them towards me, I see it's a pearl the same shade as my mother's necklace—a hair away from gray. I roll it between my fingers. *Are you my mother's?*

Scooting in a circle, I collect the pearls. Eleven total. I make a tight fist around them, maybe waiting for something to happen. When it doesn't, I carefully drop the pearls back into my open skull.

The pain comes back with a vengeance.

Seems I'm like my mother... I can't be without my pearls. Yet they come with strings.

I press both sides of my skull with the bruised palms of my hands. It's a trigger, causing the back of my head to snap closed like a bread box. The violence of bone clattering against bone churns the leftovers in my stomach.

My piano becomes a bed, my arm becomes an eye mask, and the silence the birds allow me becomes my lullaby.

wobbles.

Time has been flexible since my mother died. Since she got sick, actually. Since the fatigue started, really.

I'm in a bubble that warps and wobbles around me, making days take mere moments or forever. I was in the forest with sore knees, splitting pain, and tumbling pearls only minutes ago, but a painful night, a tender day, more days, two newspapers, and a slow afternoon have gone by. Now, I have no bruises or stiffness or new pains, a fire in the living room crackles wildly, and stir-fry is on the stove, nearly cooked.

warm.

Soft yet bristly fur scrapes against my palm. When I walked by it, the mouse loomed in my vision. Retrieving it has shown that it's but a teeny thing.

They were taken too early. If only the frost had waited another few days, this little creature could have put on the weight to survive. Instead, they'd only managed a small pooch.

In an alternative reality, I'd knit a sweater for them. They'd go to Great Mouse Beyond in the warmth they weren't able to create in life. But in my reality, I cannot knit. Nor do I think I'd be able to manipulate a small animal body.

Beside a worn round stone with a *K* scratched into it, I place an unmarked oblong one and make a grave.

I dig a hole about twelve inches deep. Using only my hands and a stick has made this more work than it ought to be.

It takes however long it takes.

The sun has shifted by the time it's large enough. Under my layers, I'm too warm. At some point, I rolled up my sleeves. A crisp breeze is now creating ice crystals from the sweat along the hairs on my arm. I watch them crack and glitter as I shift and worry because I can't feel the cold anymore.

I bury the field mouse.
Tears spill down my cheeks as I pat the dirt down.
Even birds find reverence, allowing silence in this moment.

56

difference.

In the hush of the afternoon, the sound coming from upstairs is loud. Not a crash or thud or shatter this time. The house witch is hard at work—turning everything into a siren, assuring I won't miss anything. And, being that I'm not always fully present, that seems more than possible.

I haul myself up from my cocoon.

Were there always ninety-nine steps to the second floor of the house?

Peeking my head into the guest room, it's almost a relief to see the window open wide. A pudgy black cat with one golden and one green eye sits in the center of the window sill.

A fully snow white patch coats their nose and mouth, as if they've been sneaking powdered doughnuts. The pattern is unlike anything I've seen on a cat, resembling the vitiligo a friend of mine has. Her lost melanin creates organic shapes with soft edges all over her skin, from neck to toe, and large freckles on her right cheek.

There is a splotch of red beside the cat that streaks straight to the bed. Lying on the 70s pale pink and teal comforter is a silver-blue fish with a bite taken out of it. Its dead, milky eyes follow me as I approach the cat with outstretched arms, palms down.

"Hey there, little one," I coo. That's how one should speak to cats, I was told.

A friend of mine tried to bring home a stray and wound up in the E.R. from a swipe at her thigh, a caught claw, and three angry marks that oozed blood into her tennis shoes. *I moved too quickly*, she said in defense. *If I had kneeled, dropped my voice, held my hands out... If only...*

That cat scampered off, presumably to join the other cats in her neighborhood that showed up now and again.

This little silky fur cocks their head like a serial killer. With a different intent, they would be.

Loud purring emits from their soft body. They hop down gracefully and saunter towards me. A rub on my shin, a tail wrapped around my calf, another purr that makes its way into my bones. From above, I see a celestial patch that runs down their spine.

They turn to leave, as if only here to deliver the present.

Despite the dark nature of the gift, I feel welcomed. A gesture of affection with no expectation of reciprocation from a small predator.

Without a pause, the cat jumps back up to the window sill and leaps out.

"No!" My throat shreds as I rush to the open window, expecting to see something I'll never unsee.

Heart racing, I scan the ground below.

The cat is already sauntering off, tail high and curled. *Safe and sound.* I nearly gasp with relief. I wouldn't have been able to cope.

I take to disposing of the fish and washing the comforter.

Blood isn't something that can sit. Not sure carrot soup is either, but an orange stain is better than a line of brown I'll always remember came from a dead fish.

I've been washing the soup-stained comforter over and over again for weeks now. I just keep forgetting to dry it. There is something about the repetition that's so normal now, just me washing bedding.

     ELIZABETH MITCHELL

I set the other comforter on the dryer, damp and musty smelling again, and start the machine with the new one.

Heading back to my current nest on the couch, I almost run into the cat that just leapt from the window. They are sauntering out of the tucked-away kitchen. Their tail smacks against the door.

The cat meows.

How did they get in the first time?

Too interested to understand the gravity, I didn't question things, sense the fear. This time is different. I envision a space under the house, a small bunker of sorts. It has a small window that's now in pieces. There are eyes down there, the ones I feel on me now and again, the ones who broke the lock and took the oar. So human of me, trying to put everything together.

The cat meows again, as if to keep me from spiraling.

"It's you," I say.

They meow.

I can't think of them as just any old cat forever. I'll need to call them something, if they're going to be around. And somehow, I think they will be.

Are they male or female? How old are they?

My bones say *she's* not so young, not so old. A doorframe pops, as if the house witch agrees. Who am I to argue?

Kneeling, I hold my hand out, let the cat smell me. Her eyes flick up, and an image of me splashing alcohol on an open wound enters my mind. *Any mammal can be the type.*

After a second, she rubs my hand. There is kindness and curiosity. Neither the hesitation nor paranoia I feel is reflected back to me. I doubt I'll be in any need of bandages.

She bounds past me and rushes out the back door—which is cracked open.

The sight gives me pause, sends a shiver down my spine. But I can't remember locking it, and some cats can push things. I've seen them shove things from the middle of tables so they'd crash to the floor, slam cabinets for attention, open doors because they wanted to.

I wonder if Vitti has a family or had one.

The realization that I named her is fleeting. It's right, normal, her name all along, maybe.

Stepping outside, the wind has picked up. Leaves flutter along the ground as if being kicked.

I want to go after her, kidnap her and bring her in, make her mine. I saw no collar. But she's already disappeared into the trees again. She'll need to come back on her own, settle on the couch of her choosing, declare this her house and me her... something before I will claim her, before I will encourage her to eat canned wet food instead of fresh salmon or steelhead, try a litter box, or get a cat door for a cat who doesn't need one.

"Come back sometime," I shout towards the forest, hoping the wind will translate the words, make them feline, and deliver them to her.

It would be nice to have someone to talk with. Or we could sit in companionable quiet. I miss that just as much.

unstable.

Part of my leaving the house today is to work on the canoe, but I also hope to see Vitti again. She hasn't come back yet.

The canoe is still sitting on the old blanket in front of the boat shed. I expected nothing less, yet tension releases from my shoulders.

I drop the bag of stuff on the ground and pull out Lois' instructions.

1. Remove gunk. Take a blade and scrape around the area to cut any broken fibers or gunky resin off. There may not be any of this, but if there is, just get the big bits.

2. Sand area. Put a mask on and plan to leave it on for a while. This is where you get to the nitty-gritty, so to speak. Use the 80-grit sand paper to get the rest of the gunk off. It'll still be a bit scratchy, but as long as there are no more bumpy areas, you'll fill in the scuffs soon enough.

I like Lois. She's clear, not stuffy, and managed to write *a lot* in a short amount of time. Or was I at the hardware store longer than I thought?

As I tug at the small blade's package, my fingers throb. I gnash at it with my canines, with my molars, with my two front teeth. Primal feelings well up in me as the sharp plastic nicks my lip.

I should have brought scissors to open it. After more chewing, there is a hole big enough for me to tear at it. Once I pop the blade from the molded plastic, I slide the respirator mask over my face, let the straps snap at the base of my head. The scent is sweet, pink sterile soap, wood oil.

I kneel and rub my palm across the small crack. There's a very minor raised bit. It takes little effort to cut it off.

Touching either side of sand paper turns my stomach. I pull on gloves meant for a later step and clench my jaw. The latex isn't enough separation.

One minute of sanding later, the area is smooth yet scratchy. *This makes sense.*

3. Cut repair patch. Use your new blade and cut a carbon fiber patch bigger than the crack. Be careful to do this on a surface you don't mind wrecking, in case your blade goes through quicker than you think.

With so many steps left, I won't get much further today.

I place the sheet of carbon fiber on the cement floor of the boat shed and start slicing.

One side.

Two sides.

The sounds are almost relaxing.

The third side is tougher, as if it's thicker than the other sides. It's my hands, though. My fingers are beginning to seize around the plastic handle of the blade.

It slips out of my hand and slices at the sheet. I drop it in time, so it doesn't slide through skin, into muscle and bone.

If that's not a sign, I don't know what is.

Clicking the blade back into the plastic sheath, I try to pat myself on the back for what I've done. Dad would say that Step 1 was opening the boat shed, so I was on Step 9 or something.

Best to leave the bag of tools and materials in the boat shed, save some energy for later.

I open the creaky doors for the second time in decades. It hasn't become something else—still a time capsule.

I hang the plastic bag from one of the oar hooks but barely step away before the handle rips. Everything clatters to the floor.

The urge to walk away and deal with it later is as strong as the moonshine my first boyfriend gave me at the beach. Just like then, though, I have to fight my urges, make the right decisions—walking away, in that case; staying, in this one.

Piece after piece, I collect the bits and bobs Lois picked out for me. I remember her counting when she looked at the receipt. I'm missing one item.

It's slid under the life preservers. I step in further and crouch down.

Something far more important than tape catches my eye. It's nearly hidden by the canoe storage and darkness. The sun hasn't demanded the attention she has everywhere else.

An imperfect circle about four feet wide has been carved from the shed. Jagged edges have created angry metal teeth.

I should close the double doors, buy a shed with a padlock, walk away. With little money to throw at the problem, I'll probably have to replace the shed wall myself. So I can't turn away. I lean in.

Kneeling now, I see why the hole blended at first.

Night lives on the other side. Silent crashing waves in the dark, a moon illuminating the ocean foam, sand dunes with moving beach grass, a starless sky, birds waddling on the sand, smoldering and blazing fire pits spaced out like land markers. *The night I first collapsed.*

An onslaught of emotion hits as the devastation of that night comes back, fresh as ever. I knew it wasn't just a trip, wasn't just a one-off. I'd been feeling it. Energy was in short supply, *exhaustion* and *tired* and *worn down* were no longer strong enough words for how I felt when I woke up. Weakness plagued me. My body was filled with something heavy. Standing upright felt like a miracle.

But the beach heals. So I took a weekend. A refresh would fix it all. *I was facing burnout*, I lied to myself.

On the first night, I went for a walk on the sand.

The breeze was warm and salty. Seagulls called to one another. The water was cool and alive. I, too, felt alive. It wasn't long before my legs gave way under my weight, with the inability to adjust to the movement of the sand.

My journey started then. Numerous doctors' visits. Tests. Medications. Progress. Crashing. Progress. Crashing. A new norm. A house-of-cards marriage mirroring my legs on the beach, unable to hold itself up any longer. Everything was so unstable. Almost a year of it.

It nearly broke me.

My current body gives way like it did then, and suddenly I'm folded, flopped between spread legs and bent knees. I don't hear a crack. Like the canoe, I'm supposed to be able to withstand a lot of abuse. Or so others have told me.

Heart nearly ripping through my throat, I turn back to the ocean, to the—hole in the boat shed. The sun has appeared now, and she's bouncing off the forest floor through the metal wall.

Just another thing to fix.

I grab the tape from the ground, holding back tears. I wasn't ready for that.

alone.

Rain beats soft earth as storm clouds hide the oncoming sunset. Bullets of water bounce off the metal chairs on my back patio, and branches bow under the ferocity.

I wanted to check on the canoe, go on to the next step, use the little energy I had to move the project forward. *Wanted* to.

Avoiding the cold pellets that would bring me to my knees, I make a tea and sit by the window, watch the rain soak the ground —nourish and drown in equal measure.

Hours pass, and Mother Nature cries herself to a peaceful sleep. Squirrels peek out from their hideaways, birds shake their wings and escape leaves that were solace only moments before.

Standing, I am as heavy as a flower's center as it tries to hold the rain.

Though I want to join life as it wakes, step outside, experience the breeze, I find myself unable for fear I will only sap the last bit of Autumn color from the world.

Keeping eyes on my socked feet, I retreat further into the arms of the house.

Nestled in the big chair—the one I think of as Pop's, even after all these years—I avoid the world and open Dad's birding book once again.

Flipping through the pages with the speed of a turtle, I trace beaks and say the names of birds out loud. I cherish the swirls of Dad's smudged fingerprints on the glossy paper, flecks of dinner he ate alone, and pages bent to birds he was still looking for.

Today, I hear him read the notes I didn't notice the first time around. Taking in what he spent so much of his time doing, I'm bringing him back to life.

So many birds live in Oregon. Big, small, tubby, thin, fluffy, sleek. Some have talons. Others, like my friends in the clearing, have feet so tiny they might not even leave imprints in wet sand.

I come across a photograph I could have taken myself. The two birds that sat with me on Dad's bench were Black-capped Chickadees.

I thought I didn't need to know, didn't care, would just get to know them, meet them as beautiful creatures in the woods. Yet here I am, listening to the baritone of Dad's echoing voice tell me about what they eat, their migration patterns and nesting cycles, and I want to know it all.

Maybe I'm more like him than I thought.

 ELIZABETH MITCHELL

disappeared.

A knock at the door draws my attention. It's different here. I can open the door. I can.

When I glance out of the peephole, I see nothing. Even the wind is absent. Leaves are where they were when I had a tea on the swing this morning. *Or was that yesterday?*

Opening the door speeds my heart up. *It won't be like that Thursday.* One day, I won't think of that when I'm alone and reaching for a door knob.

Creaking, the house witch makes herself known.

The windy path leading to my mother's—*my*—cabin is empty.

I quickly look around. Only when my eyes reach the stoop do I know it wasn't a knock, it was the Tuesday thud. The newspaper has come again.

My teenage ghost was quick this time. Seems she's learned to toss the paper while riding, like in the movies.

I let out a breath, revel in the calm air, and wonder how it can be Tuesday already.

The days have disappeared like morning fog. I recall snatches of time and moments that assure me a week has passed. That, at least, makes this all less disconcerting.

entangle.

A loud sing-song beep alerts me to the comforter being done for the fourth or fifth time. *It's always the noises.* I keep missing the window to dry it, coming back to damp fabric already growing dank.

Legs slightly numb, I'm slow and deliberate about walking to the machine.

How long has it been since I worked on the canoe? A week maybe? I'm still so tired, as if the little sanding I did was a marathon of one-armed rowing. It only got worse the day after.

I lift lead-lined bedding from the steel drum and drape it over my less fatigued shoulder. It drags behind me, bringing grief's cleaning negligence with it. My cane catches on a piece of flatter fabric to my right now and again, tripping already weak legs. If only I could get from Point A to Point B without it. *Not these days.*

I remember when my ex-husband and I used to go dancing. Hours of sweaty bodies colliding—mine, his, hers, theirs, others. I'd forget Joyce for a while, become someone with fewer inhibitions and more power, who was sexy and desired and loved.

Glancing down, I see frumpy clothes, a hidden body, restraint and sadness and fear.

But I left Seth because I wasn't truly desired or loved.

I was someone who tried, someone whose needs went unful-
filled, who wasted years of her life, who has been left alone
because she has a cane and a hole in her heart. His bouts of rage
are almost a footnote in the slow death of my happiness. *Almost.*

There's power in choosing myself. I just need to convince the
most irrational part of me of that.

I'm breathless from the weight of the wet comforter and the
work I have ahead of me.

Outside, I shiver as I move towards the right side of the
house. The sky, though pale gray, shows no sign of rain—a fleeting
concern only occurring to me now.

Nearing the clothing line, the temperature begins to rise. A
painting unfinished, the late Autumn sky directly above me
becomes blue and bright. The large patch of grass under the
clothing line acts as a barrier for the rich day of Spring tucked in
the tail-end of Autumn.

Around it, the world remains unchanged, with dead leaves
coating a dry ground. Inside, the grass is lush and vivid. Thin,
stringy clouds remain in the cold, while cotton balls move happily
in the heat.

I have to stand on my tiptoes to use the clips.

A smile breaches my face as my mind conjures an image of
Dad lifting me up. Even after all these years, I still can't reach.

Once the blanket is pinned and there is no fear of a gust of
wind blowing it away, I slide off my shoes and socks and squish
my toes in the plush grass. It's soft against my sensitive skin.
Warmth from the earth replaces the usual itch and burn the
blades often cause.

It's as if nature wanted to share with me a glimpse of her glory
before the cold comes in earnest.

I lie on my back, pretending I'm in a movie where people
watch the sky and talk about life. No matter that I'm alone.

Clouds race each other, desperate to make it to the other side
of the bubble they exist in. They are only round puffballs until I
picture them as something else. A bunny or shoes or an unusual

     ELIZABETH MITCHELL

house surrounded by a gate. My mother's smile. My father's dimples.

Tears stream down both sides of my face, dripping into my hairline.

Oh, how memories come. Bricks to the face from boys with gap-toothed smiles. Pushing against my desire to curl, to retreat, to run, I force my arms out to my sides as if I'm swimming and become weightless.

I float above the ground, skin hovering above the patch of green, the fabric of my oversized sweater dangling and pooling under me.

One deep breath, two, three, and my heart thrums.

Overwhelm hits—from the grief to the love to the bigness of the past.

Four breaths, five, six, and pressure builds up around the muscle that aches and breaks.

Seven breaths, eight, nine, and *pop*.

A thin vine releases from my rib cage, through loose weave.

Vibrant, green, and alive, the plant climbs towards the sprinting clouds. With each inch, my pulse slows by beats a minute.

Once it's taller than I can reach, branches the color of arterial spray grow from it. One by one, they thicken as they lengthen and bend with the weight of themselves. They begin to entangle.

Each breath I take now is more measured than before, as if I've forgotten how to inflate my lungs.

In the millisecond after an inhale, my heart stops beating. Without the heady beat in my neck, exhaling is loud and comes out in a rush.

A latticework heart emerges from the woven crimson branches. Two four-leaf clovers sprout from aortas.

On the inhale, both snap off and fall.

I catch them, and they land face down on each of my middle fingers. With my thumbs, I fold the stems into themselves. Then, I crush them.

As the plant matter smears, my parents shout from the lake house. They call my name, say that dinner is ready. I don't turn my head, too mesmerized by my new growth. Shattering glass follows, and I laugh. *Not another imaginary broken window.* The house witch is hard at work.

I breathe in tandem with the wind and lose time willingly.

After a while, the blue above me bruises. Encroaching purple hangs low over my heart made of sticks. The color thrusts me back to an old satin nightgown my mother loved so dearly. Once again, my eyes water.

As if the world is melting on rewind, an untangling begins. The movements of the branches and vines are soft and wild and rhythmic as they unmake.

I lie a while after my heart enters me again. Pleasantly warm air chills as the familiar beat picks up where there was only breathing.

The sky is only glitter by the time I settle into my wholeness again.

     ELIZABETH MITCHELL

blank.

Knees against my chest in my comfy chair, I've got the book from my mother's bedside table in hand. She was reading *I Never Stopped*. Grief and wish fulfillment and ghosts. I started from where her bookmark was—about halfway through.

I spend the night crying and finishing the book. Then, I start from the beginning to see what I missed.

I don't remember eating. But a plate slick with olive oil is empty, and a chicken breast from the fridge is gone.

When I crawl into bed, I prepare to dream about screaming and loss and The Gray. I prepare to dream about Dad or my mother or Gramms sitting on the edge of my bed, trying to get back to me.

Instead of counting sheep, I flip through memories of the large roll of school paper my mother bought from a garage sale a long time ago that I stumbled on when looking for a fresh towel set.

Half-used and bent at the edges, it cost less than a dollar. If only they'd known what she could do with it, they might have charged more.

Over the years, she found so many uses for it.

One.

Wrapping presents in an assembly line; my mother cared little about appearance. She already bought them something, after all. So as long as the receiver couldn't see inside, it was fine.

Often, the paper was crinkled and resembled the bag she used the during panic attacks we were supposed to pretend she didn't have. It would collapse and expand, collapse, expand, collapse, expand, before she would smash it into a ball.

Two.

My mother created diapers for my ham sandwiches.

Comically large, they broke apart as I walked to school. By the time lunch came around, I had soggy, squished bread and a wad of ham; the cheese had slid away, turning the mayo and mustard into a smear on the paper.

Three.

Standing in the kitchen, my mother swaddled fresh meat for the neighbors from someone's hunt—I still don't know whose. Pink dripped from the edges of the paper and in a line along the linoleum as she handed it to me and told me to deliver it quickly.

I thought I'd never eat meat again.

Four.

Strips of paper were taped in lines along the dining room to *spruce up the house.*

My mother painted fleur-de-lis and other elaborate designs on them because she couldn't stand the sight of the stained white walls. Using roll after roll of frosted tape, it looked messy and never lasted long—a week or two, at most.

That was for the best. She tired of them easily.

     ELIZABETH MITCHELL

Five.

A massive sheet of the paper was under us both. In our oldest clothes, we were ready to get messy.

We started with large brushes meant for baseboards to make swirls or splotches with the slate gray, stormy blue, Easter green. Little bits of white and butter yellow popped up like the daisies they reminded us of. Eventually, we gave up being clean and stuck our fingers and hands into the canisters, tipped them over onto the paper, and let globs and dribbles of wet drip in chaotic blobs.

From there, it was flowers. *Only flowers.* My fingers were almost detached from me as I mirrored my mother, making looped petals and angular leaves.

Hours later, we called the piece done. We didn't think of what it would be as a whole, how it would dry, what the wood floors underneath would look like after house paint soaked onto its face. We only knew it was done and that our tummies were grumbling.

I'm getting so sleepy now. The floor beneath my bed frame strains and groans.

Six.

Gramms taped a piece of the paper as a backdrop on the wall.

Together, we grabbed from a tall stack of black construction paper and created our stories. Our shadow puppet performances were legendary—or so we told ourselves.

Forests for fairies to rule. Wolves to stalk through the trees. Castles for princesses to live in. Ghosts to haunt them. Celestial bodies for dragons to dance around. Cows and plants and houses and light posts and unknown objects for the town below.

That's the last sheep I need. I roll on my side like the paper itself, and my mind goes blank.

handle.

My mother's vanity has always felt untouchable.

Sleepy thoughts of her drew me here the moment I woke up. I knew it was time. But standing here, looking at a collection of tiny glass bottles and jars, I am out to sea. These are her things, and she's *gone*. My being here is so invasive. *Isn't it?*

Small perfume bottles fascinate me. Though each is unable to hold even a quarter of an ounce of liquid, they are crafted with more care than most practical bottles. The cobalt blue glass with gold accents makes sense here on the polished cherry wood. I pocket the bottle. It will look nice on my night stand by the glass ball lamp filled with unique bark found by the lake.

Off to the right is a jar filled with colorful pieces of paper. The ribbed lid is cold between my fingers. I set it gingerly beside a silver tray that has a handheld mirror and wooden brush. Inside, the papers are revealed to be stamps from all over—Ibiza, Dallas, France, Haiti, Portland, Janes, London, Gatlinburg, and more.

Seeing all the places I've lived, all the places I've visited, in this way snatches my breath. In my young discovery phase, I traveled. Five roommates and no car in Hoboken for two weeks. Three roommates and a beat-up truck I borrowed from a neighbor in New Orleans for a month. Couch-surfing and bus rides.

Each city comes with so many stories. So many end with me leaving parties early or sleeping through brunches, fighting with my mother over the phone as I swiped on lipstick a shade too dark for me or crying because I thought I finally met someone good, but it ended as quickly as it began.

Did Mom collect these—listen to every story, every drunken ramble, every excited conversation, and buy a stamp—to commemorate *my life?* Small bits of paper with adhesive on the back, that's all they are. Yet there is a weight to them.

Their presence is heavy. I want to set them on fire.

She could have just said something. Anything would have done. Stoicism, though—that was her way. Stoicism or irritation.

The moments of love and sweetness are dreamlike, imaginings of a starved child.

I thought I could handle her room, but I've barely looked through the top of her vanity, and I'm losing it. Could have started with something less personal, but it is what it is.

The need—*thirst*—for a drink hits in a way it hasn't since I was in college. The burn of a smooth bourbon, the smack of a tart cocktail, the bite of a bad wine, whatever.

Downstairs, in the living room, my grandfather's cabinet held a whole bar. My mother dusted the bottles even though neither she nor Dad drank much. I imagine something there will suffice.

Downstairs, in the living room, my grandfather's cabinet *no longer* holds a bar. Far from it. His decanter still sits on the top shelf of the cabinet. Three cut-glass high ball glasses rest beside it on a tarnished silver platter. She kept his most cherished pieces, at least.

The two lower shelves are crammed with games I asked for all year round. Birthday wish lists included 1000-piece puzzles and Scrabble, while Christmas lists included Monopoly and Sorry! and Aggravation. We only had a deck of cards and Life, courtesy of a neighbor who took pity on me. It wasn't about money, *no.*

     ELIZABETH MITCHELL

It was about me having better activities to entertain myself with. I could play the piano, do homework or anything *outside*, use my imagination, bike to friends who lived miles away.

I pull out Connect 4 and take it to the dining room, trying not to be angry and bitter. *Who were these games for? Who got what I wasn't allowed to? Neighbor children? The paper girl? Ghosts?*

Setting up the game, I look at the empty seat across from me and nod to no one. I can use my imagination. I've gotten good at that.

unsure.

Noises outside draw my attention towards the window.

Then, I dare to dream—*Vitti?*

I haven't seen her in a very long time.

I hoped she would saunter back in, find a cushion to sleep on and knead, claim me as hers. By now, I'd be buying cat food. Unless she prefers the bugs and rats I've never seen despite forgetting to put food away for days.

Glancing out, an American Crow with a large cookie-cutter wingspan soars across the brilliant afternoon sky. I watch their methodical rowing until they disappear into the blue.

Bringing myself back to the glass, to the sounds that drew me here, almost feels like a chore. The two Black-capped Chickadees are here, tapping at grimy streaks.

Hello, there. Go to the lake. They speak without speaking, tell me I must see the sky, visit the water.

Though I'm unsure I have it in me today, I listen all the same. Dad taught me that one never ignores a bird when they tell you something.

I often wondered whether he meant literally or figuratively. Now, I know.

panic.

I'm paralyzed at the door. The exhaustion hits, tries to take me down. Knees bend, back weakens. Solid oak floors will bring only pain with my collapse.

Grabbing hold of the sliding glass doors, they groan with my weight, and my arms shake. The house witch is unhappy with the tugging. *I am not sturdy.*

Easing myself down to the floor, I stare out towards the water, imagining it through the trees. But from the first floor, I'd have to inhabit a winged being, see through their eyes as they swooped and swerved across the glassy surface.

Or I could just *go*.

I grope for my cane and nearly tumble to my side, tangling in my long knitted sweater. Hauling myself up is arduous, and I move with the same speed my mother did when she walked back from the pier twenty years ago.

With each step out, a memory hits:

Three years after, I was ready to swim again. I asked my mother to come sit on the pier. Vitriol was hurled at me at breakneck speed. She was so *disappointed.* I was *pathetic.* I *didn't love him at all.* Following her back inside, my head hung low.

Seven years after, I told her I'd like to try. He would have wanted to see me swim on my eighteenth birthday. Her words were the same, but she couldn't seem to muster the same gusto when she called me names.

Ten years after, I didn't ask, I told. He'd be so sad that I hadn't been back yet. My mother didn't look at me, didn't speak. Her silence lasted two years.

By the time she said my name again, I wasn't Clover anymore. *It's Joyce,* I told her, having gone back to using my first name, letting my hair grow, finding myself outside the person my mother had designed.

The forest floor crunches under my trudging, my cane, my fatigue. I barely register it, singularly focused on seeing the water. I cannot appreciate what's around me now, too caught in images of Dad's smile as he waves me over to him, his hands holding my waist as I kick to keep afloat.

Wind has picked up. When the lake is finally in view, the smallest of ripples disturbs the glass surface.

It's not the first time I've seen it since I've been back, but it's the first time I've had the scent wrap around me. Remembering how large my lungs are, I suck air into the organs until I am full and allow myself to just be present with the moment.

In the shape of a cross, the pier resembles a religious icon. It's fitting, as I've always felt more at peace, more connected on the rotting, grayed planks than any place of worship I've ever been to —*any* place, really.

I slip off my knit and drop it into a puddle almost as blue as the lake itself. Dirty slippers and my wedding band go beside it. I've tried to get rid of that damned ring so many times, but my skin calls out for a replacement within minutes.

With no hesitation, I jump, forgetting that it's November and the water will be unforgivingly cold, forgetting that I'm not a person who can jump or swim or even walk down hills without pausing or planning or thinking anymore, forgetting that mere minutes ago I was stumbling.

Somehow, my brain allows me to forget that I'm not well.

     ELIZABETH MITCHELL

Or fluid.

I don't slide into the water and glide back up, smooth and otter-like; I plop hard into the freezing water. It jolts my fried autonomic nervous system.

Dad's wide eyes fill my mind. *A swimmer since the womb,* as Gramms told it, the water still claimed him.

Panic takes over, and I channel him. Lungs filled with fresh air seize. The usual response to tread water is gone, as I am thrust into shock.

My mother is standing on the pier now. I see her just before I squeeze my eyes shut. She shouts that she told me to stay inside; her voice comes in warbled under the water.

Dad is beside me as I buoy a little. He's holding my hand, and I wonder if I should just let go, sink, join him—and now her. It's crossed my mind so many times over the years.

A buzz fills my ears, and my thoughts stop wandering.

Dad is gone, and my mother's voice has quieted. Suspended under the surface, all that's left is water and a low-frequency hum.

My hair begins to move, as if the water around me is churning, though every muscle is still and I am holding my breath. It's slow, swirling towards the sky.

Tiny bubbles form around me. The sensations are akin to being caught in an undertow. Fear overwhelms me as quickly as grief and apathy had. Pain and memories are a pendulum.

Trying to kick to the surface yields resistance from heavy legs. So weak that walking to the lake was a chore, I should expect nothing less. I've waited too long, and the *deep* fatigue sets in.

Is a place considered haunted if an entire family dies there? Does it matter if their deaths span decades and milestones?

Against light water pressure, I pull my lips apart to find out. I'll know Dad more in this moment than ever before, perhaps. He never showed me anything but a smile—not when Gramms died or when my mother's best friend was in a fatal car accident, leaving her inconsolable, or when I had sunburn on my birthday, followed by the chicken pox, then a long battle with bronchitis and walking pneumonia. No matter how I acted or what happened in his life, he stayed strong, at least on the surface.

But he struggled *here* in this lake. And he lost. *Was he fatigued too?*

Water doesn't fill my mouth. I don't taste algae and earth and decomposing life. My lungs fill once again. I am *breathing*. But the buzzing grows louder.

Finally, I crack my eyes and feel no burn. Opening them, my vision is clear. I'm greeted by translucent yellow and black winged beasts. Rounded, pot-bellied little things, so delicate, I wonder if they could be popped with the prick of a needle.

I take in all I can without moving my head. Glancing down, I can tell the bubblebees aren't primed to sting. Some outline my shape, creating dotted cut marks around my stiff arms like they're a fabric pattern; others just roam nearby.

Beneath me is nothingness, only dark lake water.

Are their collective slow-moving wings and the waves they've created holding me up?

They shape into a loose swarm and fly up, towards my swirled hair, flitting along my arms, tickling my ears, shifting the fabric of my ill-fitting leggings, moving past my nose, brushing my eyelashes, and kissing my cheeks along the way.

Gingerly, I reach up and touch the locks of my hair that have threaded together. Pruning fingers meet a hollow oval, like a sugar egg filled with an Easter scene. *A hive.*

My heart beats in time with the bubblebee wings as they gather. Time slows, and I wait, hovering, listening, being.

Once they've fully settled in the hair hive, I sink. My second brain hovers above me, unable to keep up.

At the bottom of the lake, the heel of my foot touches something sharp, my toes something slippery. I listen to the persistent buzz. They're urging me to go.

My stomach finally plummets, and I open my mouth wide to swallow it like a jello shot.

Only then do I walk.

I may as well be wading through thick muck, toxic mud. Even my arms shake from the exertion. But less resistance meets me with each step.

Every few seconds, I reach up to touch the hive, feeling the strands of hair that have woven to form an object so strong insects born of bubbles find solace there. I expect a stinger to pierce my exposed palm any moment, as I press and tug to see my hair's limits, even though the bubblebees may not even be able to do that.

The longer I'm underwater, the more I want to stay with them.

But my exhaustion demands a bed, a hot meal, a roaring fire. I know what happens if I ignore my body's needs. At the very least, the house witch will have opinions.

I hunch in the water as I grow closer to shore, unsure if my bees can survive out of the lake. When hunching isn't enough, I crawl. Finally, the semi-forested area by the pier is steps away, and I can no longer stay in the water.

My hair falls, collapsing the hive and the bubblebees within it. Swiveling in all directions, my eyes scan the water to see if I was wrong, if the bees managed to leave the safety of me in time. But *no*. They've left this world.

A small sorrow settles beside my many other losses.

Slowly, I gather my duds from the pier and head towards the sliding doors.

The click of my cane keeps the bees alive a little. From a surrounding hum to silence would have been deafening.

soon.

My two bird friends are on my back doormat. They trill when I get close.

"You're still here," I say. Wet leaves trail in my wake. Still, I tell them, "I went to the lake."

One of the Black-capped Chickadees bounces. The other tilts their head quietly. Part of me wants to name them Anne and Henry.

The smaller one flies up and settles on the handle of the sliding door. Nodding to the house, I say, "I really need rest."

Both fly and settle on a branch in the tree where the watching eyes live, that comes to life when I sleep, that haunts me because I fell from its arms when my mother locked me outside to spite me.

Oh, the things one remembers.

"We'll chat soon."

lava.

When the paper comes, I realize I haven't checked the mail in a
while. I don't think I collected it this week, but maybe last? I've
had letters with my mother's name on them in my hands a few
times since I've been here, but I'm unsure how many.

Being just at the end of the driveway, slippers or shoes seem
unnecessary. I'm in fluffy socks and a blanket wrapped around my
shoulders, which is becoming my signature look.

Through the thick material, the chill of the ground is not
wholly unpleasant. Until it is.

It doesn't take until the end of the driveway for it to burn.
The ground is red-hot coals, moving lava, the side of an erupting
volcano, molten glass.

I don't remember opening the mailbox, but I must have.
Because I'm standing in the kitchen waiting for my tea water to
boil in a metal kettle I think my mother had when I was a child. A
stack of mail two-inches thick is beside me.

I hope most of it is junk.

days.

It's as if they've been waiting for me to catalog them. They've been coming in pairs, in clusters, on their own. It started this morning.

While I mixed milk, egg, and butter into flour and baking powder, a collection of robins, wrens, and sparrows met on the kitchen windowsill. While I poured batter onto the griddle, more joined, and their chirps filled the house. While the pancakes bubbled, poofed, and cooked, two American Robins stole the attention, singing a sweet and beautiful duet. While I sat and ate, my company took to watching me.

Wind-ruffled feathers on the heads of fluffy birds. Sun brightened even the dullest gray bodies.

My back hurts now; I've been in one position for too long—sitting, by the looks of it. The pancakes are cold, many have been eaten, and the sun is in a different location. New birds are here; others have gone.

I've lost time again. But this time, I wasn't alone.

Long shadows play against the bare kitchen wall. Following

the dark shape of frenetic wings from a large bird determined to fit on the windowsill, my eyes land on a new wall hanging.

I don't need to stand to see it, but I can't read the plaque beneath it.

Down to the broken hairs on the left side from sleeping wrong last week, the head on the wall is my twin. Her eyes—*my eyes*—are closed. Lips are more relaxed than I think mine have been in a while.

The wood around my mounted head is cherry, I think. It's polished and smooth, shaped like a coat of arms.

I have to get fairly close. With the bird shadows moving across the wall, the thin script is near-invisible at first.

When my forehead is nearly brushing my chin, I see it reads, *Joyce. How much time has she lost?*

I step back, my curled hand presses against my mouth. No one can answer that.

Sliding back into the kitchen chair, I pick up my fork to take a bite of pancake. It's the last bite. My orange juice glass is empty, and the birds have all flown away too.

I take my empty dishes to the sink, trying to discern if I'm still hungry. Rinsing the plate off buys me a moment to think, but I still can't tell. Another decision for later.

As I go to leave the kitchen that has nothing for me, I notice that my mounted head is gone too.

Everything is gone.

Everyone is gone.

     ELIZABETH MITCHELL

exhale.

I only took a short nap. But now, glancing out the window, I see only darkness.

The sky should be as speckled as Vitti's back, filled with sparkling dots making angular shapes, transformed into figures by mythology.

Tonight, every star has disappeared. Only a deep violet ink remains.

Making my way downstairs, I try to turn lights on in front of me, but they deny me, and I'm left blind.

Outside, the backyard flood lights are also gone. No matter how many times I flick the switch, I'm only practicing an exercise in futility. The night has eaten all 2,000 lumens.

I grope my way to a chair on the patio.

After being here for so long, I'm surprised their location isn't second nature.

When I touch the metal arms, I slide into the seat, regretting the lack of cushion within seconds.

Do I exist in a moment unable to be seen? It's like a sound in the woods when no one is there to hear it. I know, but also, I'm unsure, and there's something so peaceful about that.

Goosebumps blossom as the wind picks up. The usual rustling doesn't follow.

I wonder if the leaves are moving, or if they have also ceased to exist. *Has the darkness stilled them?*

I remember the first time I cried because of a monster under my bed. When I peered under, pushing the bed skirt aside, there was nothing—nothing but pitch black space.

The socks I kicked under there earlier in the day were gone. My recorder and spare notebook and missing chapstick and lime green ponytail holder and the plastic bin of holiday decorations my mother stuffed under because it wouldn't fit in the closet—all gone.

Fear in that moment was inevitable. I was vulnerable. I was unprepared for the unknown.

In this moment, *that's* all gone.

Swaddled in this state, I'm small, but everything around me is wondrous. More foreign, and yet...

Breathing is easier without me seeing my chest move—deeper and purer. *Doesn't ache.* My lungs fill more than they ever have. I imagine they are pink balloons stretching past their limit.

When I exhale, it's as if my breath is filtering through the long exposure of a camera. An auroral display pours from my mouth and trails up towards nothing. The light is neon green and pastel yellow with purple hues fanning the edges.

I am a celestial body. My bones are mere sketches connecting the stars that shape me. One could see right through me, pausing only to wonder how I'm held together with so little.

My next inhale takes longer than the last.

I suck up the darkness, fill my connected balloons with black and violet and deep sea blue.

On my exhale, I am *undone.* And slowly, the world around me changes.

One star. Two stars. Three stars pock the sky, as my very being relights the sky.

Four, five, six, hundreds, thousands.

     ELIZABETH MITCHELL

Nothing of me remains, which happens when one is swallowed whole.

But for once, I don't stay shattered. I don't need months to put myself back together.

After the pieces of me are taken, after the night sky becomes a fierce spectacle once again, molecules of me collect. I'm space dust. I'm fireflies. I'm light particles. I'm atoms and cells and organs and blood and flesh and bone.

belong.

Drawn to the lake again already, I want to spend more time there. Would my bubblebees reappear if I jumped in? Or would the freezing water claim me this time?

I leave the comfort of my sunken couch for the bitter cold of the forest.

Frost develops on the edge of my sweater sleeve, soaked from a tired wrist giving way while washing a pot. I would have thought it dried hours ago—even the streaks of soapy water I left on the counter have.

I curl my fingers into a fist and crunch the crystals away as my cane bangs against another frozen branch.

It's December, only a little too early.

A squeak to my right draws my attention. Soft brown fur peeks out from a cluster of rotten leaves. From within, a bunny emerges. We lock eyes, and I know. In the wild is where I belong. Even when my bones ache, even when my skin burns, even when my legs shake, I'm more at home in my poorly insulated cabin and wandering in the trees than I ever was in Janes or any other place I've lived. Similar to a wish fulfillment romance novel, I've found my place. Unlike the escapism of love, though, I find more solace alone.

Rustling in the bushes puts both me and my furry friend on alert. A fox, perhaps. Or a snake. Maybe a bird of prey settled on the forest floor, primed to nab something small.

My thoughts go to the mouse. I should tend their grave—tend all the lost ones' graves. *When did I last do that?*

With the same suddenness they appear, the bunny whips their head towards the noise. They dart off before either of us can catch a glimpse of what's out there. A small patch of clover reveals itself from where they'd been sitting. The right corner of my mouth tilts up, and a tiny snort from my nose leaves a poof of air in front of my face.

I continue my trek, moving slower in case the *something* would scare easily enough to see me as a threat—me with my cane and my too-large boots and the symphony of a crispy forest floor.

Lois' instructions await me, as do my mask and more gloves. I'm proud that I didn't leave everything on the ground, setting myself up for success before walking away last time.

I read over my next steps, stopping at the most natural place.

4. Mix resin. According to the package, mix one full plastic cup of resin. It's a one-to-one kind of thing.

Easy enough. That's not a real measurement, and I'm often better with descriptions, rather than numbers. It's why I've always been a better cook than baker.

5. Paint the resin on the damage. Use a lot of it. Let it sit for ten minutes to make sure it doesn't need more. Do steps 6, 7, and 8 immediately after this step.

6. Reinforce with Kevlar. That's the sheet you cut. It gets laid on top of the resin.

7. Cover the area with release film. Think of it like cling wrap. You want it smooth and taut.

8. Cure. You need to walk away for 72 hours. Just let it harden up.

I can do all of that. I've just got to convince my frozen, seizing hands and muscles of that.

brutal.

Mid-morning, I'm lost in watching an ant crawl up the wall in a swerving pattern. My heart pangs. The little searcher is so far from food, it will die before it eats. I could squish it, save it from starvation, from pain I'm not sure it feels, but the smell its crushed body would trigger my gag reflex from across the room. On my skin, remnants of the scent would cling to me for days.

With my back flat on the thin carpet, legs kicked up on the pale teal wall, a slip of wind creeps through a broken weather strip on the floor and sends a chill into my bones. My long-sleeved shirt isn't enough. All of my sweaters are by the full washing machine. I just did laundry, and yet it's piled up already. There's only one of me. *How is that possible?*

Without thinking, I glance up towards my mother's bedroom, as if I can see through the floor into her dresser. I'm sure she has something fluffy and warm—that would smell like her and bring me to my knees.

I resort to wrapping myself in a blanket. And for a time, I'm warm.

But when I need to make lunch, it becomes a hindrance. I find myself slumping, the knit fabric heavy on my shoulders.

Opening the refrigerator is the final straw.

My forearms are shocked by the cold. The little heaters aren't keeping up with Mother Nature. Real roaring fires are a constant necessity now, and it takes a toll to make one.

Crawling up the stairs has become so commonplace I am in awe of the days I can walk up every step without hunching or dropping to my knees or taking long breaks on every other step or grasping the lifeline one might call a railing.

They are never ending when I'm tired. Funhouse-like, they stretch and mock.

Reaching the top of them always makes me want to swivel around and say, *"Thank you, thank you. It was hard, but I got there in the end."* Awaiting crowds at the base of the steps would cheer and throw flowers, naturally.

But not now. At this moment, the quiet almost hurts.

Standing outside of the door to her room, I raise my hand to knock again. *I'll get used to it eventually.*

I remind myself I've done this. I've been in here since she died. I've investigated. I've walked out with my head held high.

The house witch makes herself known again, making the scuffed wooden floor groan under my socked feet.

The door opens for me before my fingers touch the tarnished brass knob.

My mouth bones clatter together. Though she's not here, my mother's presence fills the room as I head to the five-drawer oak dresser Gramms gave her.

Third drawer, if I remember correctly. The top is *unmentionables* and socks. The second is shirts. Sweaters are next. Then pants. Finally, a drawer I've never opened. Today is not the day to address that.

I tug the third drawer open and see that nothing hasn't changed. Grabbing the closest sweater, I end up with one the color of a stormy sky. It unfolds as I pull it out.

My current shirt reeks of uncertainty, pain, fatigue. Mothballs and a hint of my mother's perfume may be complicated, but it's an improvement, nonetheless.

In the hallway, I shuck off my top, and a childhood song about the floor swallowing me whole flits into my head. I tuck the rumpled tee between my knees so it doesn't fall to the ground.

I slide the sweater on part of the way.

Prickly rayon wool scrapes my arms, my face, my chest. Like low-grade sandpaper, it leaves abrasions along the tops of my ears.

Gasping, even cheetah speed wouldn't be fast enough as I try to shake it off. My shirt tumbles to the floor, but I barely notice with the overwhelm of sensation.

Miniature toy soldiers holding weapons march out from the sweater's weave. Dozens of them litter my skin in a whisper of time, their arms swinging in unison.

The sleeve catches on my wrist, and small faces screw up. Straight-backed molded plastic arms raise bayonets.

I have to get this off now.

Yanking the itchy fabric over my hand is brutal. The toys pierce me with tiny spears. Blades stab into the tops of my hands, the meaty pads of my palms.

Lift and stab. Lift and stab.

I twist and shake my wrist, fling my arm around wildly. They fly across the room, hit the walls. Each melts into a shadow.

But there are so many left, still marching across my chest, their weapons catching on my bra as they poke and prick. Some crawl along reddening forearms or drag their heels against my swelling cheeks.

Droplets of my blood are left in their wake.

I smack at them, squish them into raw skin. The blue of their clothes and silver of their weapons smears with the red of me. Eyes watering, breathing shallow, I am a pointillism painting in progress by the time I've killed them all. Sweaty and panting, I trudge to the bathroom.

I tell myself that it wasn't that bad. *I'm fine.* It wasn't the worst material I've had touch my skin. I think about the fact that I needed to shower.

The house witch lets out a high-pitched squeal as I turn on

the water of the bathtub to the hottest setting. Perfect hot cocoa temperature comes out instead. She won't let me burn myself.

Before I jump in, I crack the window open. It'll make the water colder, but the fresh air will calm my nerves.

Passing by the mirror, I see no puncture marks, no bits of squashed soldiers. All evidence of the attack and death is gone—a battlefield two hundred years later. All that remains is me. Dark ginger hair that's grown so long it's become flat, with unruly bangs brushing my eyelashes. Though they hide a scar that reminds me of the night I realized my ex-girlfriend was not worth another tear, they also hide my favorite constellation of freckles. A droplet of sweat clings inside the sightly cleft chin that can be seen time and time again on Dad's side of the family.

The stench of my body begins to fill the steamy room. I turn away and step into the shower.

lumps.

Wearing a thick, fluffy blue towel, I waddle to my current bedroom. It's quiet. The birds are sleepy or elsewhere. I could use music. The fatigue is hitting hard, though, and I'm unable to handle memories in this state.

A chill brushes over my burning skin, and I cry out into the still air. In my room, I notice the window is wide open.

After I close it, I check the latch three times. It's sturdy, solid, unable to open itself.

I pull on a soft tee that won't end in bloodshed and thin pajama pants. A twist of my damp hair leaves it in a knot at the base of my neck. I brush my bangs to the right side, unsure if I'm training them or biding my time until I cut them.

With lumps in my ponytail and clothes that won't keep me warm, I am human again. There's no energy for perfection today —or any day, really.

Perfection is something I'd always strived for. At my firm, I was the top-performing lawyer, but things are different now. I'm working on that part of me—the part that insists on smooth hair and flawless eyeliner, no mistakes, who thinks sleep is for the dead. I want to have flyaways and a bare face, to enjoy my happy accidents, and sleep when my body tells me to.

I jumped at the chance to leave Janes, and that was one of the reasons. Secretly, I knew that. I just couldn't admit it.

Some would argue that it's a big city that feels more like a small town. But it demanded more than I had to give—or maybe who I surrounded myself with did. The city may have asked nothing more than for me to wake up, do my job, go to bed, rinse, repeat. No energy to unpack that now.

Shaking off thoughts of a life left behind, I head back to the living room.

gone.

Washing my face, a *thud* shakes the downstairs. I peek out of the small circular window and see the newspaper girl.

Tuesday again already.

So many days gone.

Cerulean graces the late sky and reminds me of the canoe.

I wait until even the back wheel of the girl's mint and cream bike has disappeared before I step away from the window.

I crave an early morning row onto the lake, my breath puffing in front of me, mist hovering above the glass that ripples only when my oars move the water.

When I touch the spot I covered with resin, I'm pleased that no squish greets me. I assume it's dry.

9. Remove release film. It should pull away fairly easily.

OPTIONAL:

10. Smooth with sandpaper. This isn't the most necessary part, but if you want to fix any ripples, this is when you do it.

11. One more coat of resin. If you do sandpaper it, you'll need to coat it with resin again.

I guess it's done. Should've read the instructions all the way through and I'd be prepared to go on the water now.

I'll just go back and change, bundle for a slow paddle across the lake.

From behind a tree, a familiar furry body emerges.

"Hey, Vitti." My heart swells. "It's been a while." A long while. "How are you doing?"

Her loud mew with a tall tail tells me she's doing alright. *I think.*

Chilly wind whips my hair behind me and takes me out at the knees. It's so fast, I barely realize it's happening. I clutch my cane, but it's not enough. I can't hold myself up, both arms are being moved by the intense breeze.

But *no*. It's not the wind.

It's fatigue—fatigue hitting so suddenly, it's almost unreal.

Collapsing on the ground, damp leaves soak into my marrow.

Vitti curls beside me and purrs so loudly my skin vibrates. Her speckles resemble white berries scattered on the forest floor. The comfort she brings me shatters the wall I held up for no one but myself.

Tears come. From pain. From exhaustion. From fear. From loss.

They're warm on my face, so I leave them for a while. After five or ten or twenty or one or two minutes of sobbing, the tears slow and grow cool. I am weary.

I must wipe them away, must crawl home, must eat and sleep and try again tomorrow.

Touching my face is unusual. There are no tears to wipe away, only soft grooves melted into my cheeks, culminating into globby puddles on my chest. I reach for the top of my head and am disappointed to find no tiny flame flickering.

Vitti licks my waxy skin without hesitation. The roughness of her tongue is grounding.

"You're right. I have to get up," I tell her. "Now if only I could reach my cane."

As if she was meant to be with me at that moment, she stands and moves towards it. She nudges it with her forehead inch by inch. It reminds me of my rabbit when she'd apologize for scratching. What a beautiful soul she was. And what a beautiful soul Vitti is. I love that she's here once again, even if it's only for a little while.

The second the cane is back within reach, I grab it and begin the arduous process of lifting myself.

"Thank you, Vitti. You're such a good girl. You know that, though, don't you?" I right myself. "You can stay with me anytime, you know? Just wanted to let you know that," I add.

She saunters beside me as I limp, slow and measured, to the house in silence, enjoying the natural ambience around us.

evaporated.

On the couch, I am a sculpture of fatigue. Over two hundred bones are posed in the fetal position. Sheets of skin drape over top to create a shape resembling a woman.

Two memories come to me in this moment:

Falling asleep in the sun, only to wake feeling drowsier than before I'd closed my eyes.

Jumping in the lake wearing a sundress, and drenched fabric weighing me down.

Unable to lift my arm, I know that the top layers of me were soaked overnight, made heavy as they sucked the water molecules from everywhere else in my body, in this room, the glass that was full last night.

The bottom layers laid out in the summer sun elsewhere in the world. They dried out. As I baked and burned, the rest I expected evaporated.

My mind is alert, no brain fog in sight. *What a curse today*.

I close my eyes with the little strength I can muster and will myself to sleep. It won't help, but it'll pass the time.

alight.

I dream of loss.

I'm five or six, my mother and father hold my hands as we walk along a sidewalk. In front of us, a park with a pink curly slide and a purple dinosaur rocker. My father lifts me when we get close. His arms stretch long enough he can place me at the very top of the slide. Pushing off, I shoot through the tube and go around and around and around. Light streaks in through the connected pieces. The loops seem to go on forever. Until, they don't.

When I finally reach the bottom, my parents are waiting, arms outstretched. A hole in the sand opens, and they fall into darkness.

I scream, but a laugh comes out.

My skin is alight with pain and electricity dancing across nerve endings, burrowing into my muscles when I wake. Moving makes me wonder if there's an invisible vice around my ribcage.

Opening my eyes is akin to skinning my eyelids.

Darkness surrounds me, and I worry I fell into the gash in the ground. Reaching, I touch the walls. Tiny fibers scrape across my fingertips.

I'm in the blanket—small, as if I'm watching myself lose my parents again.

No, smaller. Only inches tall.

The fabric is impossibly heavy when I push at it and try to claw my way out. Weak, tired legs slip on the soft bedsheets as I struggle to escape the puddle of my clothes.

I lie back, trying to find solace in the fact that I'm alone. No one will scoop me up and toss me into the growing pile of laundry or brush me onto the dirty rugs or put me in the way of rain boots and canes.

done.

Though I lose the morning, the afternoon, and into the evening, I am my five foot something self once again. It happened slowly—inch by inch. As the shadows on my wall changed shape, as the room went from dark to light to dim, I grew, joints aching and skin searing.

Even at my normal size, it takes a while longer to crawl out from under the covers, to feel human.

My stomach grumbles—a reminder I haven't eaten since yesterday afternoon. My legs burn—a reminder of my romp and tumble in the woods. My back throbs—a reminder I haven't stretched in so long.

I manage to see my way to the kitchen before it's dark.

Leftover chicken and noodles are in the fridge. Scarfing them down quickly makes me swell.

Cramps rear their head as I'm considering my lack of control and wondering if that had anything to do with a high school friendship falling apart.

Acid in the back of my throat and nausea join the fray. Instinct sees me putting the kettle on and reaching for bottles—antacids, anti-nausea medication, gas reducers.

To keep my mind busy, I wash a few dishes. Every other motion causes the sponge to scrape my skin off. Even an attempt to wipe up the dirty counters causes a gasp. *Guess these are Tomorrow Chores.*

I putz.

A stray dish makes its way to the cabinet, the salt shaker gets moved to its rightful place, I throw an errant paper towel away.

Unable to wait for the six-minute timer to go off, I call my tea ready early. The calm is more than necessary.

Steam hovers above my under-steeped cup of chamomile. Despite that, I reach for it. The landscape of my tongue burns like a forest on fire. *Fuck.*

Half of me wants to drug myself to sleep, the other half craves proper distractions.

I look at the floor. It could use a sweep. Though it's slow going, I get up some bits of leaves and crushed cereal that have been there for a while.

My tea is no longer steaming, which means two things: I've been in here too long, and I can take a cautious sip.

As I leave the kitchen, I enjoy a luxurious gulp of my perfect temperature tea.

Seizing intestines double me over.

The mug slips from my hand and crashes to the floor. I step on the edge of the broken handle as I rush to the bathroom. New pain ripples up through the piercing in my foot. *It's too much.*

Something hard, unyielding, and forceful starts to come up and clog the back of my throat as I lift the toilet seat.

Pills. Two, three, seven. Edges of the compressed powder rub the insides of my mouth raw. Ten, fifteen, eighteen, more. I lose count of the white oval shapes. I lose time and space, and I am wrecked.

The purge turns to a dribble. Eventually, I'm spitting stray pills onto the pile that fills the toilet bowl and forms a mountain.

When even that stops, I watch the mound of pills turn into a soggy mess.

     ELIZABETH MITCHELL

Dragging myself to the couch to curl up, all I can think about is how today needs to be done.

still.

Waking before the sun, I am empty and spent.

The water whispers to me, as if knowing I need to be healed. My canoe has been ready and waiting, as have I. And now, in the stillest of hours, we have to wait no more.

I thought I closed the boat shed door, but when I arrive it's wide open and empty.

At the lake's edge. I experience the words more than hear them.

Crunching loudly, I make my way to the water to see a fine mist hovering above it.

At the lake's edge, beside the dock, my patched canoe is beached on dirt and dead leaves. *How* it got here seems unimportant at the moment.

As if I'm sliding a silky dress or well-worn sweater on, I slip into the seat and sigh. It's been too long.

Across the bow in an x-pattern, the oars await my weak hands. I grab hold of them and use one to push myself away from shore.

Sloshing joins the far-off bird calls. Above me, the first quarter moon hasn't quite disappeared in a mauve sky. Fatigue tells me I cannot go far out, revel in the wet air and soft sounds of the water, breathe in the beginning of a new day, as I want to.

It takes most of what I have to propel myself forward a few times.

I stall out after four strokes. My mind wanders to my bubblebee friends. Are they underneath me now, waiting to be recreated? If I fell in—or jumped or slid—would they arrive? Or would I be lonely, lost to the water as Dad was?

Trying not to shift my body too much, I glance to my left, down into the water.

No bubblebees. No fish. Nothing but me.

Not just me—a reflection aged and lined far beyond the years I've lived. I am frail, gray, covered in soft folds and freckles that have shifted with elongated skin. My aged self becomes Gramms. She smiles at me with the same sparkle that telling stories always gave her. Her face smooths, goes back in time, becomes my mother's. Stern, with love hidden behind the hardness, she blinks when I do, tilts when I do. *I miss you.* Another blink, and she melds into Dad—his rugged face, five o'clock shadow, wry smirk. *I love you.* He ripples to a girl of seven or eight that I almost don't recognize. Almost. She shakes her head independently of me. I blink, and my child self melts back into the woman I am today.

I sit up, crack my neck, wipe wetness from my cheeks.

My body barely notices me rowing back towards the dock. Tugging the canoe from the water, though, feels impossible. As if it's all caught up to me, I have little energy to get the canoe to a place I'm sure it won't slide back in with a strong wind.

Taking a moment is necessary—walking, moving, getting to the house cannot happen if I don't encourage my body to resettle like the house I live in.

I stay as still as I did the morning a doe emerged from the trees and grazed in front of me. Yellow rays cascaded over her as she nibbled flowers and grass. My presence did not perturb her until I moved. Primal fear took over then. If only I'd stayed still longer, allowed her to finish her breakfast.

Stillness is the answer to so much.

jelly.

Cool sunlight floods the guest room. One corner holds a brass pharmacy lamp with a halo of dust motes. The opposite is the only space in shadow.

On my left is a small closet with slatted shutter doors.

Once, it held monsters. Then, Dad, who was always bad at hide-and-seek. Later, clothes meant for donation that never left the house. Now, I don't know.

Forest green silk wallpaper with a feminine pattern of lemon yellow and bubblegum pink flowers and chartreuse leaves is peeling in spots to my right.

I'm reminded of my mother's decorating attempts. Gramms didn't change things up because she was bored, though. What a difference permanence can make.

Sun-bleached in spots, a large oval mirror hangs dead center of the wall, giving the illusion of a smooth transition from pale and exhausted to bright and untouched.

Gramms hand cut hummingbirds from a book and glued them on top of the silk. Their beaks faced the flowers. They hovered in mid-air. They tilted impossibly by the base of a leaf.

It's the most magical of walls. Her favorite bird immortalized

in the room she shared with people she loved. Must be why I feel
at home here.

I recognize the local Anna's Hummingbird. Pink heads signify
the male. The Ruby-throated Hummingbird has oil-slick green
feathers, which only make the red of the male's chin appear
brighter. The less colorful hummingbirds across all hummingbird
species are female. Just being alive is enough to attract attention.
That's complicated to me—beautiful in its simplicity, problematic
in its purpose. But that's nature. Simple and focused on survival
by any means.

Today, I am a hummingbird. I am focused on one thing—
trying to survive. I'm doing nothing in order to be human again. I
can only be complicated and multifaceted and filled with nuance
if I rest for a while.

Time gets even more slippery when staring out of a window in
a cozy bed.

I'm only aware of it when a helicopter breaks the occasional
trill or chirp or caw. It's far off, but noticeable.

Wracking my brain, I can't think of a reason for a helicopter
to be nearby except an accident.

My heart grows heavy with the thought of someone being
airlifted.

Something whizzes past my vision. Then another something.
More somethings.

I glance at the wallpaper with leaves and flowers and remnants
of glue outlining shapes of birds made mostly of air.

Gramms' hummingbirds flit around the room, bouncing excit-
edly. Over a dozen of them.

Some seem to have gotten stuck being flat, as if someone
forgot to blow them up. Those hover close to the closet, as if
ready to attach themselves to the smooth yellowing door if they
aren't made whole.

Sitting up is hard. Whether it's because my body wants to be
jelly or because I move so slowly in fear their pointed beaks might

        ELIZABETH MITCHELL

pierce me, I'm not sure. The result is the same: sluggish muscles. I may as well have been running, pressing weights, doing hot yoga.

I slide my back to the white wicker headboard, crushed and understuffed pillows coming with me.

The hummingbirds spin and twist around each other. Unlike in gardens, where they often flap each other away to have sole access to sugar water or the brightest flowers, the wallpaper hummingbirds appear to be playing, enjoying each other's company, flying together as if they would never dream of being competition.

After a while, I yawn once, maybe twice. My eyes flutter slow. With each long blink, a hummingbird or two disappears.

When I wake, the hummingbirds have rejoined the wallpaper. All but one.

Perched on the lamp in the corner, glitter dust now falls on her metallic green feathers. She is mostly shades of gray.

I sit up slowly, and she doesn't move. I stretch. I yawn. I shift. I stand, and she doesn't move. I take a step in her direction, and she doesn't move. I walk closer. I reach my hand out. I coo, and she doesn't move.

The little helicopter flies towards me and lands on the bunched fabric near my forearm, wings moving at a speed that creates only a shadow in the air.

I whisper a name like a question. "Gramms?"

She flutters away in a blink. But I know I'll see her again.

aches.

Stretching, I find myself regretting the decision to stay in bed most of yesterday. Unused muscles ache. The fatigue is worse, as though I overdid resting. What a balance I teeter on.

A small snore alerts me that I'm not alone. At my feet, Vitti is partially hidden by a sweater I must have shucked off in the night. Her face is tucked into her chest, and she's holding her legs straight out. A little shrimp.

Shifting the covers to get up almost makes me feel guilty. Luckily, she doesn't wake. Could be that it takes me five minutes to turn my body and another five to slide off the edge of the mattress and touch down on the ancient rug.

I slog through washing my face and brushing my teeth. I nearly fall down the stairs. Oh, how happy I am that my royal subjects aren't there to jeer. Today, only the house witch is here, making each step creak as if the wood might crack under me if I don't step quickly enough.

Getting from the bathroom to the kitchen is *hard*. But food doesn't make itself.

With arms made of metal, I crack eggs into a pan, pour orange juice into a clean glass, and grab a fork. *All set.*

Vitti's turn.

Before I am halfway through peeling a tin of tuna open, she materializes. Her fluffy tail whips back and forth, smacking my leg hard enough that I wince. The flicking switches to hitting the floor. A light *thump, thump, thump* tells me she is talking to me.

"What's up?"

She saunters towards the back door.

"You want me to follow you?"

If Vitti is anything like that yipping Chihuahua that led me to a mugged college kid years ago, she is taking me to something important.

Imagine if I chose to ignore such a sign, shooed her out. Whatever message she had for me would be lost forever.

The stove clatters as if I'm jostling the racks. What is the house witch protesting now? Going or staying?

"One second. I need to get some shoes on," I say, pulling my frying pan from the stove and turning the burner off.

An impatient trill snaps back, but I zombie-shuffle away.

Once I'm as winterized as I can be in a matter of two minutes, I ask Vitti. "Where to?"

She marches straight out of the house towards the lake.

Following her, I'm slow. She takes a sharp right before the pier and disappears into the woods.

Shafts of butter yellow light beam through the canopy. I try to keep pace with Vitti, but she darts ahead, then waits for me. The deeper I go, the more cluttered with dead foliage the forest floor becomes. My rain boots are instruments, creating a soft squelching and crunching symphony in cadence with each step I take.

Birds chat to one another above me, just out of view. Dad would have known them by their songs—high-pitched or squeaky chirps, the occasional throatier squawk. Every once in a while, I heard him mimic their sounds and would have sworn they responded to him. Perhaps I'll be able to do that one day too.

     ELIZABETH MITCHELL

Could be that Dad was speaking gibberish at them, though. *Leaves eat sky, and worms coming. Storm trees in the lake. Beware!*

The sun yawns and warms and shifts to a pale orange.

Vitti meows once to let me know she's still up ahead.

I've been walking for so long, my heart races and my breath is short. I didn't remember our woods being this large. *My* woods.

Eyes drooping a little, I know I can't go much further—not if I want to make it back, not if I don't want to make the forest my new home. It was just morning. I'm sure of it.

There's a clearing, much like Dad's. Vitti sits in the center of it. Beside her, my mother's jewelry box is open.

The four-leaf clover ring sparkles from within, as fake gems often do.

"No," I say aloud. "No, Vitti. It's not time yet." *It may never be.* "Take it back."

Vitti stretches in response. I want to take that as a *yes*, but I know it's not one. She circles the box and sits right back where she was.

"No."

I can't leave until I know the box is safe, and she knows it. So I have to wait until she takes it back the same way she got it here.

Looking me straight in the eyes, Vitti's only fully black paw reaches towards the box. She winds her arm up a little as if she's going to strike a bug or rat.

"Vitti..." I warn.

She swats the box with the hidden strength house cats have, and the jewelry box careens across the empty space.

My mother's prized possessions tumble out and into small clusters of leaves.

I gasp. The word *why* is another piece of jewelry spilling out onto the ground as I collapse.

Vitti moves to me and rubs my arm. It takes everything in me not to smack her across the clearing, treat her like she treated the box. Instead, I shift away. *She's just a cat, and I am not a monster.*

"No. I don't want your affection." Grief makes the words harsh and guttural, my voice coming out thick. "I just... Please go away." On my knees, I'm pleading, I'm begging, I'm praying. I hate myself.

She's just a cat, but...

Vitti moves to the edge of the tree line furthest from me, but she does not leave. I don't have the strength to say anything else.

I crawl to the jewelry box first and grab it. Leaf dust clings to its pearlescent pink satin. The small inside mirror is intact, but only two pieces of jewelry held on during the journey across the clearing. The remainder are strewn out. Collecting them aches. Each piece brings a new memory, a moment with my mother.

The seashell charm: her kissing my scraped knee at the beach. Her tennis bracelet: a screaming match about Dad's absence in our lives. The lapis broach: my first night alone in our other house. The heart charm: when I told her I had fallen in love the first time. Her first engagement ring: a story of another man, another time, another her, a timeline that could have been.

Then I come to them, side by side in the center of the circle I'm in.

A chirp grabs my attention. Behind me, two Black-capped Chickadees are flanking Vitti, so like Mom, Dad, and me. We were unusual. A ginger, when they were both brunettes. Sad eyes and a downturned mouth, when their faces rested pleasantly, a little happier than neutral. Only my cleft chin points to me being in the family.

A petulant child, I snap at my only friends. "I'm doing it."

The simple gold wedding band sits squarely in the middle of her pearls. Without looking, I know the wedding band has an inscription. Mom showed it to me whenever she felt grateful for Dad or the loss was so great she couldn't help but lacerate herself open to ease the swelling pain.

"for my wife & our daughter"

I cannot touch it.

     ELIZABETH MITCHELL

I lay my cheek on a patch of twigs nearby. They stab into my flesh, and my eyes water. I need to be close to them. I need to rest. I need to be anywhere but here.

My eyelids flutter, exhausted by this moment, and I breathe in the scent of earth and animal and oncoming rain.

Instinct.

I drift off to a place beyond daydreaming, but not quite dreaming. Lightbulbs are rain drops falling from a sky filled with doors open to nothingness.

Hands press through walls, warping the house witch to have wallpapered balloon skin, stretched in shapes over wooden beams.

Animals watch from just outside the guest bedroom window. Owls hoot, sharing stories of grief, of my loss of family, body autonomy, friends, husband, job.

It just is, the first says.

She can survive, the second replies.

If only she knew.

She'll figure it out.

When? She'll never heal.

Soon. Soon.

Are you sure? the first asks.

Be patient, the second replies.

A burst of cold fills the bedroom, and I wake before the sun, worn down and sweaty.

Vitti is curled around my mother's closed jewelry box, settled on the pillow beside me.

Careful not to touch her, I ease it open. Every item is accounted for.

Stretching hurts, so I allow myself to stay frozen here, with Vitti's quiet snoring as my lullaby.

After a nap or two or just a moment of dissociation, the view from my window disappears. A pale, cloudless gray sky bleeds into thick mist. Barely distinguishing itself from anything, the ground is a vague dark shadow below it all.

I know what lies beyond my home, yet its new absence makes my backyard foreign, like the starless night. This house of grief is an island in a sea of white.

Vitti jumps up beside me and chitters. *Who is she talking to?*

"I'm going out," I tell her, grabbing my sweater and heading downstairs.

Vitti is not as curious as the adage claims. She stays at the back door, I think. I glance behind me and see nothing. The house is but a vague silhouette, and I have lost sight of her entirely.

The fog coats the forest like a dream. I can't see inches in front of me. My own arms cut off at the elbow, half in a portal I can never fully move through. Spin around twice, and I'd lose my way home.

Instinct leads me to the pier—an instinct I lost when the world went dark. Standing at the edge, I itch to jump, to crash into the still blue lake and rise to a sandbox world. I want to be surrounded by the ghosts that live on the fringe of everything, hide in the white nothing space.

Is this *The Gray* from that book my mother was reading?

The only legend Dad ever told me was that when the sky was obscure, souls could roam and touch our world once again, moving through liminal spaces with no barriers.

If true, I wonder what would happen if I wandered with them. Would I vanish like they did? Could I find my way back? *Would I want to?*

I stay on the pier until the heavy mist has dissipated and the sky returns. Sirens have not beckoned me, nor have souls offered me a path. Dad's voice hasn't echoed across the water's surface. My mother's face hasn't appeared in the mist. Gramms' weathered hands have not reached from beyond.

Still alone, I go back to my house, knowing the house witch will be active, settling—her wood groaning, doors swelling and sticking. All will be normal once again.

esophagus.

Lying on the cross-shaped pier in the early morning is a religious experience. The only sounds come from nature and beings that were here long before humans and will exist long after we die off.

Morning breeze flushes my skin, makes me breathe with more intention, and rustles what's left of the leaves. The lake sloshes against the wooden pilings in a rhythmic pattern. My eyes have threatened to close, despite the sun's waking.

Fresh air fills my nostrils. Birds fly overhead, and I briefly wonder what they are.

I haven't screamed since he died twenty-eight years ago. I've shouted and raised my voice. But just screamed? Made a sound that rippled through the air for no reason? Allowed my lungs to decompress so fully I became breathless? *No.*

Yesterday was Tuesday. I realized only when I went to get the mail and saw two papers on the front doormat. More time lost.

This morning turned so quickly.

One second, it was peaceful. The next, I was ready to break the wood floor beneath me in half with my teeth. I haven't allowed myself this feeling in a long time. To ease the pressure, I came here.

I feel connected to something bigger when I'm outside, when

I'm by the water, when there is an open sky. Even more so at my pier.

So many years ago, it feels like a dream, I was visiting a friend's church. The girls had long braids and wore skirts that hid their ankles.

After a part of the sermon, she reached over and grasped my arm. "This part gets strange."

A woman jumped up, taken by the Holy Spirit. She spoke in gibberish that reminded me of trying to make up a language as a kid. *If we say, "Ungurhla,", it means "we're best friends".*

Today, the first Wednesday in December, I will be the one crying out in tongues, wailing in the center of *my* church, demanding attention.

My soul will be lifted as I purge loss after loss after loss after loss after loss after loss.

I pull myself into a standing position with my cane's help, because it is something I should do with my whole body. With my toes curled around the edge of the pier, I release.

My attempt at screaming starts off weak, as if I'm trying to interrupt a conversation in a loud restaurant. There's something awkward about screaming for screaming's sake. Though I'm utterly alone, self-consciousness grabs hold.

I swivel around, wonder how many birds are watching.

Time moves by me, and I settle into the moment. I suck in the deepest breath I can and open my closet filled with baggage.

I get *angry* for myself, for my losses, for the overwhelming grief, for the grief I've not allowed myself to feel. Having to leave my life and not doing it sooner is heavy in me. I'm mad that I stayed with an abusive man, loved an abusive mother, couldn't save Dad. My fatigue disappoints me, brings fury to the back of my throat. That first collapse, the second, the one yesterday, my skin's sensitivity, the nerve endings of my fingertips—it all hurts. It all pisses me off. As does the fact that I haven't screamed before today. But above all, I'm angry for my fragile heart going through all of this *alone*, even when people were holding my hand.

Starting deep from within my belly, rage collects, clings, forms, moves up. My esophagus burns with its need to escape.

Raw, husky, animal-like, a loud shout bursts forth. A high-pitched cry takes over and shatters the quiet.

Clusters of wings burst from trees, cawing loudly.

They mimic. They match. Maybe they mourn too.

The ferocity of my scream doesn't stop. *I* do not stop. Heat flushes my cheeks, and I glance towards the water's surface.

Joyce, as I know myself, is gone.

Obscuring my head completely is a cotton candy shaped plume of fire. Shooting up from my sweater, the flames that have replaced me dance, as if they are my scream.

Vitti brushes against the exposed part of my ankle. I can't pause to wonder when she got here. But her presence softens the edges of my pain.

Rain starts as a sprinkle. A cold drop slips down my ring finger. Another falls onto the back of my hand and settles. And another, and another. The smattering causes ripples across the water.

Then, all at once, the lake is bouncing. A shower has arrived. Petrichor replaces animal and fresh grass. The temperature falls.

On the undulating surface, I watch my blaze recede.

By the time the visage of me I've seen in mirrors countless times is all that remains in the water, sounds of a house fire rise from behind. Wood crackles, glass shatters and beams crash through the floor. A life burns.

One tree catches, and like dominoes, the whole forest goes. There's no heat as my woods burn, and it takes only minutes for the inferno to dissipate—a mere flash fire that leaves nothing but silence and stillness behind.

Spent, I head towards home. The forest is alive and dead, dull and vivid, dank and bright.

Vitti's tail is high in the air as she runs ahead of me. Clearly, she's enjoying the arriving sun that's already begun to dry the earth.

JOYCE

Leaning heavily on my cane, I trudge towards a future, a past, a present, an unknown. The cabin, the house witch, and the forest have withstood my anger. But there is still destruction to be tended to.

Joyce, as I have come to know myself, is unfinished.

Chronic fatigue syndrome, allodynia, and dissociations are featured heavily in this book. It's important to note that they do not show up the same for everyone. Joyce's experiences are an amalgamation of my own, those of people I know, spoonies I've spoken to about the topics, and research.

Symptoms vary from person to person, but the descriptions in the book are how they show up for many, presented through a realistic or magical lens.

For many, but not all, with chronic fatigue syndrome, the body becomes a heavy object that's nearly impossible to move, and the easiest activity can feel like a marathon. Thinking feels like a slog, which is called brain fog. Sleeping barely helps to keep up with the day-to-day and rarely touches exhaustion.

For many, but not all, with allodynia, the cold feels like putting your hand against a kettle. Certain fabrics feel like they are slicing or stabbing with each fiber, and even the whisper of air can make skin hurt. Extreme nerve pain can come at any time for seemingly no reason or have a known trigger. It is often, but not always, a symptom of a larger condition.

For many, but not all, who dissociate, time becomes fluid, so eating or stepping outside may be the only goal of your day.

Memories come in pieces or feel hazy, as do events from minutes ago. Feeling detached from your body is a norm, and being grounded in reality is a relative term.

If you haven't experienced these things, it may be hard to grasp sitting beside yourself and watching as you continue on with your day or the concept of crip time and taking three hours to brush your hair or throwing away half of your clothes with no regard for what you'll have left because if the fabric touches your skin, you cry.

I have but one request as *you,* dear darkling, move through the world. Have compassion and empathy for the people going through these—and the many other—very real things that are often hard to articulate. They are living through the strange and unimaginable daily.

     ELIZABETH MITCHELL

Acknowledgments

Of all the books I've written, *Joyce* has been the most fraught. It began as one thing, hurt too much to write, stalled, and had many more stumbles before it morphed into the realistic and magical story I love so much.

There are people I have to thank for that in different ways.

Valerie, thank you for showing up for the 12,000 word brain dump that this book was in its very first iteration. Before the order made sense, before I felt the movement or growth or understood what I was saying, when I only had the bones and some meat, you read and *saw*. It means the world that you felt the power of the story.

Katherine and Laura, your insights showed me I was doing what I wanted. I appreciate you both for your honesty, your thoughtful questions, and your time.

Erin, if I said this aloud, it would could out in a rush, all blurred together. Thankyouthankyouthank. You let me bitch about how my writing was going and how it wasn't, cry out the frustration, and listened to snippets of a story you wanted to read totally out of context. I talked your ear off about this little book, and all the while, you were just a beautiful friend, patiently waiting until it was done so you could read it in its entirety. I cannot tell you how much I appreciate you. I'm glad you're a part of my life.

To those I wrote with during the process, thank you for being a part of the journey! And to those I complained to or got very excited and told you about a version that may or may not be what you just read, I thank you too.

Thank you, artists who gave your work freely for the art used in this book. Credits are on the copyright page, but you deserve a special note of appreciation. Once I started finding the images, chapter titles changed, and the pages came alive in a new way.

Bubee, my love, I always thank you. But this time, you know it's different. You know that it's you I have to curse and to thank for *Joyce*. She's more focused, more honest, rawer than I knew she could be. Thank you for listening to me through the struggles. I cannot fathom how that was for you. But your support is how I made to the other side. I love you now and forever.

And, as always, if I missed you, I'm sorry.

If you and I have ever come in contact with one another, if I have ever seen a photo you've taken or street art you painted, if you have ever walked past me or held the door for me, you are probably owed a thank you.

So, thank you, strangers, acquaintances, friends, exes. I'd have fewer stories without you.

About the Author

Elizabeth Mitchell is a disabled author, multidisciplinary artist, and publisher who's lived many lives. Her work challenges, blends genres, explores haunted bodies, and delves into the human psyche. She's an activist, a gamer with potato aim, and an avid reader. As a woman with several invisible illnesses, she enjoys living a semi-horizontal life with her husband and spoiled furbutts in the PNW. Her writing is also under Elle.

For more, visit her website www.justanotherelizabeth.com.

If *Joyce* spoke to you and you'd like to read it for your book club, check out Elizabeth's website for discussion questions and a full book club guide.

Joyce